BUFFALO HUNT

The buffalo now stood still, facing the girl called Eagle Woman. She rode the gray horse slowly forward, and the cow blinked suspiciously, then turned to run.

The run was straight away. Eagle Woman held tightly with her knees and let the finely trained horse approach on the animal's right side. It was a difficult shot, impossible, almost. The girl concentrated on placing her arrow precisely as the brown blur of the moving form darted past. At the same time the horse had begun to drop to its haunches in a sliding pivot. Momentum carried the rider forward, over the horse's head, to crash heavily on the ground. Men rushed forward. The cow lay kicking, but the other form on the grass was still.

Long Walker was the first to reach her, cradling her head in his lap. Dully she smiled at the young man.

Another hunter rode up and dismounted. "Well," he commented, "at least she made her kill!"

Long Walker had reached the height of his tension for the morning. He looked up indignantly at the speaker. "Stupid one!" he shouted. "This is her *third* kill! Did you make three kills today?"

Bantam Books by Don Coldsmith
Ask your bookseller for the books you have missed

Daughter of the Eagle

≫ ≫ ≫ ≫ ≫ ≫ ≫ ≫

DON COLDSMITH

BANTAM BOOKS
NEW YORK • TORONTO • LONDON • SYDNEY • AUCKLAND

RL 6, IL age 12 and up

This edition contains the complete text
of the original hardcover edition.
NOT ONE WORD HAS BEEN OMITTED.

DAUGHTER OF THE EAGLE
A Bantam Domain Book / published by arrangement with
Doubleday, a division of Bantam Doubleday
Dell Publishing Group, Inc.

PRINTING HISTORY
Doubleday edition published July 1984
Bantam edition / June 1988

DOMAIN and the portrayal of a boxed "d" are trademarks of Bantam
Books, a division of Bantam Doubleday Dell Publishing Group, Inc.

ISBN 0-553-27209-8

Published simultaneously in the United States and Canada.

Bantam Books are published by Bantam Books, a division of Bantam Double-
day Dell Publishing Group, Inc. Its trademark, consisting of the words "Bantam
Books" and the portrayal of a rooster, is Registered in U.S. Patent and Trademark
Office and in other countries. Marca Registrada. Bantam Books, 666 Fifth
Avenue, New York, New York 10103.

PRINTED IN THE UNITED STATES OF AMERICA

RAD   15   14   13   12   11   10   9   8   7

Introduction
>> >> >>

By Jeanne Williams

Fictional Native American women are often portrayed as lissome maidens with apparently nothing to do but ensnare or rescue the hero, or as overworked, overburdened drudges who relieved a monotonous grind of chores by sticking burning splinters into captives or otherwise abusing them. Of course, like their white counterparts, most Indian women were wives and mothers and devoted most of their time to gathering and preparing food, caring for children, clothing their families, and fulfilling obligations to their group. However various the ways and means through which these duties are carried out, they are traditional and universal concerns of women.

In most cultures, there have been exceptions. Nuns or priestesses have vowed themselves to God rather than man and the spinster aunt appears everywhere. When we think of women warriors, however, except for Jeanne d'Arc, we usually go back to the Amazons and Scathatch, who lessoned the Celtic hero, Cuchulain. In *Daughter of the Eagle*, Don Coldsmith shows that we can find the phenomenon of women war leaders in our own American West, not posing as men as did a few adventurous whites, but as persons recognized as possessing exceptional valor and military skills.

These were unusual, true, but exist in numbers that validate Coldsmith's heroine. As children, most were tomboys, preferring bow and arrows to dolls and helping their mothers. They were not encouraged in this behavior but the evidence is that if a woman proved she had a warrior's courage, the men of her group accepted her as one, valued her counsel, and followed her leadership. This is the more remarkable in a warrior society where a man's prestige and position derived mainly from his success on raids and war parties. He might be admired for hunting skills, wisdom, or other qualities but the essence of manhood lay in military prowess. That such men could and did acknowledge the women who met their standards is a tribute to the value they placed on bravery and achievement. Though white men had numerous routes to wealth and power other than soldiering, can you imagine General Grant sharing command with a woman? It is no wonder that women warriors were usually revered as shamans or holy, for it took not only valor but a strong and invincible spirit for them to lead that life.

It was common for Native American women to accompany their husbands on raiding or war parties, usually staying in shelter though they might act as sentries or messengers and fought if the conflict reached them. Apache women frequently joined in skirmishes and James Kaywaykla related to Eve Ball (*In the Days of Victorio*, Tucson, AZ: University of Arizona Press, 1978) that his mother, Gouyen, not only fought valiantly and often beside his father, but possessed the power of never being wounded whereas his grandmother had the power to heal wounds.

Eve Ball, a valiant woman herself, gradually won the respect and confidence of Asa Daklugie, son of Juh and Ishton, Geronimo's sister, and his recollections are recorded in *Indeh: An Apache Odyssey*, (Provo, Utah: Brigham Young University Press, 1980). Like

Kaywaykla, he attests the bravery of Apache women. Both of these excellent books honor Lozen, perhaps the most famed and tragic of all women warriors.

Cousin or sister to Victorio, Lozen is the only Apache woman renowned as a warrior in her own right, the only one who was not married or took a man's part on a mission to avenge a husband or relative. Victorio called her a shield to her people, "strong as a man, braver than most, and cunning in strategy." One explanation of her choosing a warrior's life is that she fell enduringly in love with a Seneca, Gray Wolf, who stayed in her camp for a time while seeking a new home for his people who were being forced out of their ancestral lands in New York.

Whatever the truth of this, Lozen journeyed to Salinas Peak, the Sacred Mountain of the Warm Springs Apaches where the Mountain Spirits dwelled. There she fasted four days and nights, tested by the spirits who were intermediaries between mortals and Ussen, the Supreme Being. Lozen's quest was rewarded with the power to heal wounds and locate the enemy. She did this by standing with outstretched arms, facing the sky and praying as she moved in a circle till her tingling palms showed where the enemy was. At such times, her palms turned almost purple. She often used this priceless gift, when, fighting with the last holdouts, she rode with Victorio, and after his death, with Nana, and last, with Geronimo. Many Apaches believed Victorio would not have been killed at Tres Castillos if Lozen had been there to warn him of the approaching troops.

Geronimo's negotiations with white commanders were usually carried out through Lozen and Dahteste, a woman who accompanied her husband to war and fought beside him. Lozen was with Geronimo when he surrendered, and was sent to Mount Vernon Barracks, Alabama, in April of 1887. Dying there of tuberculosis, this splendid woman was buried secretly by her comrades, but I like to believe that her spirit returned to the mountains.

Like Running Eagle, the heroine of Coldsmith's book, women from many tribes sought vengeance for the deaths of loved ones. One Apache woman, also known as Gouyen, was so distraught at seeing her husband killed and scalped by a Comanche, that she slipped out of camp alone to follow the enemy. Three nights later she saw their fire, put on her ceremonial dress, and joined the merrymaking, luring her husband's slayer away from the dancers. Unable to steal his knife, she bit into his throat while gripping his arms and somehow managed to hold him till his struggles ceased. She then scalped him, stole a horse, and escaped. When a loved one was avenged, most women returned to their ordinary way of life.

Undoubtedly, a few women preferred the excitement of raiding and fighting to marriage. The Crow Medicine woman, Pretty Shield, in *Pretty Shield* by Frank Linderman (Lincoln: University of Nebraska Press, 1972), tells about a woman called The Other Magpie who fought against General Crook and his Lakota and Cheyenne allies at the Rosebud, shortly before Custer was wiped out. Pretty Shield said that another Crow woman who joined in the battle, Finds-Them-And-Kills-Them, was neither woman nor man though she wore woman's clothing and worked like one.

The Other Magpie, says Pretty Shield, was bad and brave and pretty. She had no man of her own but her brother had recently been killed by Lakotas and she rode against them that day for vengeance, armed only with a feathered coup stick. Forehead painted yellow, a stuffed woodpecker on her head, mounted on a swift black horse, she charged straight at the enemy, spitting and shouting that the spit was her arrows. She struck a warrior with the stick, counting coup on him, and in that moment, Finds-Them-And-Kills-Them shot him dead. The Other Magpie took his scalp.

It must be remembered that war honors were carefully worked out according to the hazard and difficulty of a feat. Battle, to Native Americans, wasn't so much a matter of killing an enemy as of demonstrating skill and courage. Touching a living foe, as The Other Magpie did, was counted a braver act than shooting him from a distance.

The two women also saved a wounded man, Bull-snake. When he fell from his horse, Finds-Them-And-Kills-Them dismounted and stood over him, firing as fast as she could load and shoot. The Other Magpie rode around them, singing and waving her coup stick. When the Lakotas swooped in to finish the helpless Bull-snake, she rode right at them. Her power was so strong that the enemy retreated. Bull-snake was rescued and that night there was a jubilant scalp dance. The Other Magpie cut her trophy into small pieces so that more people could join the celebration. Pretty Shield was proud of the women and it angered her that their valor was forgotten when men told of that battle.

Rare as it was for Cheyenne women to fight, enough did so to form their own society. Yellow-Haired Woman, the most famous of them, was noted for her exploits against Shoshonis who attacked her small village. She killed two Shoshonis with her butcher knife and helped defeat the raiders.

The Kutenai claim Water-sitting Grizzly, who not only hunted and fought with the men but took a woman for a wife. The Ojibwa have several women warriors, most notably Chief Earth Woman who rode to battle with the man she loved though he was already married.

In *Daughters of the Earth* (NY: Collier Books, 1977), Carolyn Niethammer tells about more of these women. Pohaha, a Tewa, was a great tomboy who wouldn't behave like a proper young maiden. When enemies approached the village, her uncle challenged her to fight them. Taking bow and arrows, she began to laugh and sing and went against the foe with gaiety and boldness, pulling up her dress to show them she was female. Tradition says she killed all the intruders and returned wearing a mask which was long preserved by the Cottonwood clan who understandably made her a war chief.

A kachina of the Hopis represents He'-e'-e, their warrior girl. Her mother was doing her hair in the butterfly style of Hopi maidens and had only one side secured when they saw enemies creeping toward the village. With half her hair flowing, He'-e'-e snatched up weapons and ran to warn her neighbors, leading them against the attackers till Hopi men could come from the fields and complete the victory. The hair of her kachina is depicted as it was that day, half whorled and half loose.

A cantankerous Pawnee won the name Old-Lady-Grieves-The-Enemy by resisting a force of Poncas so overwhelming that the village men thought it useless to fight and hid in their homes. Outraged at such cowardice, the doughty matriarch stripped, put on a loincloth, twisted up her hair, and went after the Poncas with a war club, killing one just outside her door. Shamed into action by this example, the Pawnee men helped rout the greatly superior force. Only years later did the Poncas learn that the brave old man who had shocked them into retreat was really a woman.

The Cherokees had a society of Pretty Women who had done some heroic thing or were mothers of warriors. They advised at war councils and determined what would happen to captives. Some women went into battle painted and stripped like warriors. Wild Hemp, wife of a chief, was so furious with grief when she saw her husband killed in battle, that she seized his tomahawk and exhorted the men, who were running away, to turn and attack. Inspired by her, the Cherokees triumphed.

The celebrated Running Eagle of the Blackfeet, bearing the same name as Coldsmith's protagonist, began practicing with bow and arrows at the time boys did. The first hint of her future came during a buffalo hunt when she risked her life to ride back to rescue her father whose horse had been shot.

After her father was killed in battle and her mother died, the girl, then known as Brown Weasel Woman, captured eleven horses on a raid against the Crows.

Stealing enemy horses was prestigious as well as practical, and Lozen, too, was acclaimed for her skill in this risky feat. The Blackfeet camped after their successful raid and the future Running Eagle was a sentry. Two enemies expected to easily overcome a woman but she shot one who had a rifle and pursued the other who fled only to be killed by the roused Blackfeet. This courage forced even dubious traditionalists to accept her.

Like Coldsmith's heroine, she went on a vision quest and received power. Running Eagle, a name given only to outstanding warriors, was bestowed upon her, and she was allowed to speak at the Medicine Lodge ceremony, an honor belonging to men, though now and then a warrior's wife was permitted to make an address. After winning her name, The Brave's Society of Young Warriors accepted her as a member. Never marrying, she was considered holy as well as a fighter, and assisted in giving the Sun Dance.

Comparing these actual Native American women with Coldsmith's Running Eagle, we find many common attributes and experiences which prove he has created a heroine whose gifts and deeds, though remarkable, are credible in the context of Lozen, The Other Magpie, and all their brave sisters. Running Eagle goes raiding to avenge her brother and gains the respect of the warriors who come to value her enterprise and bravery. She undertakes a vigil for power, which is granted, and, a proven leader, possesses all the qualities of a great chief.

Will she now follow the example of the most illustrious of her real-life models, renouncing marriage for warriorhood? It will be fascinating to see, in the next books of The Spanish Bit Saga, what choice she makes and how it affects her people.

Portal, Arizona
September, 1987

Eagle Woman moved gracefully around the dance arena, stepping precisely to the beat of the big dance drum. She had been a warrior sister for three seasons now, a priestess of the Elk-dog Society. Admiring glances from young warriors of the band told her reassuringly that she made a fine appearance as she fulfilled the ceremonial function at the opening of the Warriors' Dance.

Her white buckskin dress, with intricate quill work, was of the finest, reflecting her skills and those of her mother. Her glossy hair was parted and braided flawlessly, shining with blue-black highlights like the wing of a crow.

It was said that her looks were much like those of her grandmother, Tall One, at the same age. The older woman, still handsome in her maturity, was said to have been the most beautiful of her generation. She was the wife of Heads Off, chief of the Southern band of the People, known as the Elk-dog band because of their skill with the horse.

To that couple had been born two sons of distinction. The younger was now medicine man of the band, skilled in prediction, in healing, and, most of all, with the buffalo. It was said that of all medicine men in the entire tribe, none had stronger buffalo medicine than that of Owl.

The elder son, called Eagle from his earliest days, was now a respected subchief, one of the most important leaders of his warrior society. That was, in fact, how his daughter had become a warrior sister.

Eagle Woman enjoyed the ceremony, the pageantry, and the responsibility of the honored office. Besides, there were other advantages. She wished some day to marry and to raise strong warriors and capable women of the People. Yet there had been no suitor that came close to her ideals. A very independent girl, she had preferred competition with the young men rather than romance.

As children in the Rabbit Society, both sexes received instruction in the use of weapons and in athletic skills. The young daughter of Eagle had been aggressive and talented in her learning. Soon the others were jokingly calling her by her father's name, adding the feminine "woman." As names sometimes do, the appellation stuck, and she became Eagle Woman. The girl gloried in the implication and pushed harder to perfect the warrior skills.

Her masculine pursuits may have frightened away some suitors. Yet others seemed intrigued by her differences, and the persistence of one or two was becoming annoying. It was with some degree of relief, therefore, that Eagle Woman accepted the honor of becoming a warrior sister.

This position required a vow of chastity, so in effect she could decently sidestep any unwanted proposals. Her reason was the best. Her office in a warrior society forbade such activity.

There was only a slight gnawing of doubt in the back of her mind. Sometimes in the darkness, in the privacy of her own sleeping robes, Eagle Woman wondered. Was there something wrong with her? She had watched her contemporaries pair off in marriage until no woman her own age remained single. Even one of the other warrior sisters had resigned the honored office to marry.

Now, at nearly nineteen summers, Eagle Woman was the oldest unmarried woman in the tribe. Basically, however, she was happy with her lot. Her demeanor radiated confidence and satisfaction, which may have only added to her beauty.

Eagle Woman continued to step around the circle to the beat of the drum and the chant of the song, moving right to left with the other two warrior sisters. She passed her brother, Bobcat, seated at the edge of the arena, and he smiled proudly at her. He was two summers older, mischievous, and teasing, but he was obviously proud of his sister, her position of honor, and her well-recognized reputation for beauty.

The girl did not return his smile but maintained the stolid dignity of the ceremony. Straight before her and stiffly upright stood the eagle feather in each hand, symbolic of far vision and courage.

She passed others of her family as she circled. Her grandfather, the chief, sat with Tall One, both now showing the snow of many winters in their hair. The People had prospered under the leadership of Heads Off and the Elk-dog medicine he had brought from his far tribe. There were hardly people alive now who remembered a time before the horse. It was as if the Elk-dog had always been.

Eagle Woman stepped past the point where her own parents were seated, acknowledging their presence with a glance. Eagle was seated with his left leg extended before him, rather than squatting or sitting cross-legged like most of the People. He had walked with a limp since before Eagle Woman could remember. There had been a stampede during a buffalo hunt, with the young warrior swept away by the frantic animals. Badly injured, he had been missing for six moons, given up for dead. There had been strange circumstances about his rediscovery, but she could not remember. Something to do with her uncle Owl, the medicine man.

Suddenly Eagle Woman almost jumped, startled by the gaze of a young man at the circle's edge. She knew him well, had known him all her life. He was Long Walker, son of one of the chiefs of the Elk-dog band. The two children had always been rivals. On the few occasions when Eagle Woman had been bested in athletic skills or proficiency with weapons, her opponent had been this young man. At times she had hated him for his ability. Always he was a relentless competitor, keen and quick, ready to laugh at her discomfiture in defeat.

Now she read a new expression in the smiling face. His gaze was one of unabashed admiration. The girl was shocked, because she had never thought of him in this way. Long Walker was a rival, a competitor, not a potential romantic figure. She was irritated by his bold stare and shrugged him off with a toss of her raven braids. Outwardly she remained perfectly stoic, still wondering at this turn of events.

She knew that Long Walker had no wife. That was a matter of some wonderment in the band, too. He was quite eligible. Though still living in his parents' lodge, he owned many horses in his own right. His lack of interest in marriage had led to whispered speculation as to whether he might choose to be a woman-man. Still, he had not yet started to cross-dress, and he had a good reputation in the hunt.

Again Eagle Woman was irritated at herself for even wondering. What matter to her if some conceited young warrior wanted a wife or not? It was no concern of hers. She had better things to think about.

2
>> >> >>

Let it be said, to the credit of Long Walker, that he did not push his courtship too hard. In fact it may be doubtful that he considered it a courtship at first.

Perhaps it seemed to both of the young people, as they rediscovered each other, that they were only renewing a childhood friendship.

Through the Moon of Falling Leaves, the two met frequently for walks in the warm sunny afternoons. They watched the long lines of southbound geese thread across the bright blue of the autumn sky, trumpeting their collective babble of sound.

The Moon of Madness followed, and then the Moon of Long Nights. During this and the Moon of Snows, there was little opportunity to meet. Sometimes, during one of the long evenings, various families would gather to smoke, visit, and gamble with the plum stones. Then the two rediscovered friends would have an opportunity to talk.

After the Moon of Hunger, when all things began to stir in the Moon of Awakening, they found more time together. Cold Maker retreated back to his lodge in the icy northern mountains, and it was more pleasant to be outside. They could take long walks again and watch the flight of the geese on their return journey.

It is true that the things they talked about were the days of learning in the Rabbit Society. They laughed together over incidents of many summers past. They spoke of the stern discipline of their teachers, including Standing Bird, grandfather of the young man, and Long Elk, kinsman of Eagle Woman.

"Remember when we were supposed to be practicing with the throwing sticks and went swimming instead?"

The girl nodded, laughing.

"And Beaver nearly drowned. We pulled him out and pretended that he fell in and we had to save him!"

The young people would have been surprised if they had known how aware of the entire incident Long Elk had been. He and Standing Bird had privately chuckled over the way the children had handled the crisis. At one point the watching Long Elk had nearly rushed from concealment to rescue the drowning boy. But the other children had acted appropriately, and a lesson had been learned. That, after all, was the purpose of the Rabbit Society.

The couple would also have been surprised if they had seen the smiles, whispers, and nodding of heads among the women of both families. Both young people were past the usual age of marriage, and it was with a great deal of satisfaction that both sets of parents viewed this developing relationship. There was some degree of relief that the two appeared normal, after all, merely slow in developing the expected interest in homemaking.

And the choice appeared perfect. The two families had been close for generations. No better match could be imagined.

Oblivious to all this, the two principal figures continued to enjoy each other's company, as friends and equals. Their conversations, supposed by all to be

romantic interludes, were actually discussions of un-
romantic things. They talked not only of the past, but
of the present. There was certainly more of tribal
politics than of courtship in their long talks.

Both could remember the Big Council after the death
of Many Robes. It had been important because of the
election of a new Real-chief to preside over the entire
tribe. Many Robes had been Real-chief, and a good one,
as long as most of the People could remember. He had
been very old.

After his death, the chiefs and subchiefs of the five
bands had met at the Big Council to choose his successor. Both Long Walker and Eagle Woman had been
at an impressionable age during this period and were
aware of the long discussions among the People. At
the time it had been boring and tedious. The children
would rather have gone out to play. Yet somehow the
proceedings had left enough of an impression that
they had retained more than average interest.

Eagle Woman was aware that her grandfather, Heads
Off, was for a time considered for the position of
Real-chief. His foreign background, though, had eliminated him from nomination. In the end, Black Beaver
of the Mountain band and White Antelope of the Red
Rocks band had been rejected because of age. The
Eastern band, long considered foolish and eccentric,
presented no viable candidate, and the office of Real-
chief returned to the Northern band of Many Robes.
His successor was a dynamic and respected young
warrior named Rides-the-Wind for his daring feats on
horseback.

Eagle Woman had been greatly moved, anyway, at
the importance of her relative. She had developed an
awareness of family which would mean much in her
future life.

Thus she and Long Walker talked of such things,
rather than the small talk which would have been
expected in such a situation. There was talk of weapons and of the skill of young Stone Breaker. This
young man had inherited both his father's name and

his expertise in fashioning flint shards into knives, spear points, arrow heads, and tools.

They spoke of the warrior societies, now three separate organizations, which had been formed before these young people could remember. Besides the Elk-dog Society, named for its horsemen, there were two others. The Bowstrings traced their existence back to before the horse; they were the original Warrior Society of the People. This was the more politically conservative group, honoring the tradition of the old ways and usually doing their fighting on foot.

Equally respected, however, was the newest of the warrior groups, the flamboyant Blood Society. This radical, young organization had been ousted completely from the tribe a generation ago, earning its way back only through devotion to tribal loyalty.

On arrival at manhood, a young man would accompany his elders on a major hunt. If he distinguished himself well in skill and courage, he would be invited to join a warrior society, usually the one of his choosing.

"Walker," the girl spoke suddenly, after one of their long discussions, "I want to join a warrior society."

"But, you are already in the Elk-dog Society."

"No, not as a sister, I mean as a warrior."

It was at this precise moment that Long Walker was guilty of an error in judgment so far reaching that it changed the course of the history of the People. The young man could have asked for more information. He could have simply agreed, or approved, or asked why, or any one of a number of other actions.

But Long Walker did none of these relatively harmless things. He was to regret many times in the coming moons that he had had no more insight. For he did the one thing that would rock the tribal structure to its base and cause him to curse his own stupidity.

Long Walker laughed.

3

>> >> >>

It was not at all unusual for a woman of the People to participate in a buffalo hunt. Usually it was some young wife accompanying her husband in a carefree spirit of fun and games. There would be time later to settle down to the care of children and the lodge.

The People had always been proud of their women. They had a reputation for beauty, but also for athletic ability. Early training in weapons and the hunt was given to both boys and girls. Many of the young women—tall, slender, and long-legged, as the accepted norm—were quite proficient with weapons. It had been only a few winters ago that the women of the band had been instrumental in the defense of the village. The Elk-dog band had been at low fighting strength because of the political trouble with the Blood Society. Their traditional enemy, the Head Splitters, had discovered their weakness and had launched an all-out attack on the winter camp of the Elk-dog band.

The Head Splitters had also had an opportunity to observe firsthand the effectiveness of the women's

skill with weapons. The wives of the Elk-dog warriors
had defended the strip of woods on the flank, counting
many honors. Songs and stories recounted the victory
and the women's part in it.

Women of the People also held higher status than
women among some neighboring tribes. They could
own property and could speak and vote in the council.

So it was not unheard of that young Eagle Woman,
daughter of Eagle, announced that she would go on
the next buffalo hunt. The unusual aspect was unspo-
ken. Only two people knew, at that point, that her
motive was more than to have a good time. Only Long
Walker and Eagle Woman herself knew that she intended to use this hunt to qualify herself for application to the Elk-dog Society. Long Walker had tried in
vain to dissuade her, but his attempts only made her
angrier and more determined. *Aiee*, he should never
have laughed, he now realized too late.

Meanwhile Eagle Woman prepared herself for the
hunt. She practiced endlessly on her horse, riding swiftly
past and thumping a well-aimed arrow into the grass-
stuffed skin target at every pass. She had chosen the
bow rather than the lance. It required perhaps more
balance and dexterity but less brute strength.

From his place of concealment, Long Walker watched
and shook his head in despair. As a user of weapons
the girl was good, without question. In his heart he
already knew she would succeed in the hunt.

She must make at least one unassisted buffalo kill.
Then she could request induction into the Elk-dog
Society. There was the formality of acceptance, but as
far as Long Walker knew no qualified warrior had ever
been refused. It was an accepted step, a ritual progression into manhood. Manhood? Long Walker shook his
head again, frustrated and uncomfortable.

Perhaps the most distressing thing to Long Walker
was his own inability to walk away from it. A season
or two ago he would have found the situation uproariously laughable. It would still seem so, if it were any
other girl. But now, just as he and the tall daughter of

Eagle had rediscovered each other, she had developed this crazy idea of warrior status. Perhaps she had gone mad. Still, her every action was precise, sensible, and efficient—appropriate, at least, to the effort at hand. She was behaving as any normal young man approaching the time of elevation to membership in a warrior society.

And again, that did not befit a woman of the People. At the age of Eagle Woman, some eighteen summers, most were married. All other unmarried women were busy developing their skills in sewing, cooking, and preparing skins. Most girls far younger than Eagle Woman had started to collect the small items necessary for the time when they would have their own lodges. There would be the small flint knives and scrapers, bone awls for sewing, and perhaps a supply of sewing sinew.

Many girls also started very young to collect their cooking stones. Skill in choosing and use of the stones was a major factor in developing a reputation as a superior cook.

Perhaps Long Walker should have felt more secure. Deep in the storage space behind the lining of Eagle's lodge was a small rawhide pack belonging to his daughter. For many seasons the girl had assembled items to be used in her own lodge.

But Long Walker had no way to know the womanly instincts of this young woman. He could only see that she seemed to be behaving in a very unfeminine way. This was affecting the young warrior deeply and in strange ways.

First, it seemed that the girl was becoming more attractive and desirable to him. Perhaps it was only inaccessibility, but he felt increasingly drawn to her.

Then there was the matter of concern for the girl's safety. Long Walker found himself increasingly anxious that she would find herself in a situation of great danger because of her masculine pursuits. He felt an urge to hold her, to protect and shelter her from harm. Wisely he refrained from any move in that direction.

He realized that in her present stubborn frame of mind it would only make her angrier with him.

There was a very real danger in the offing. He was not concerned with the immediate physical danger of the hunt. Long Walker had confidence in her ability to handle that. But, if she succeeded and applied to the Elk-dog Society, the next step was the fast and the vision.

Each warrior, before formal induction, must go alone to a remote place. With no human contact for at least three days, the aspiring warrior would spend the time in prayer and fasting, seeking his vision. It was during this time that he would find his spirit guide, his medicine animal whose identity he must never reveal.

Long Walker had gone through this religious rite two summers previously. It had been a deeply satisfying experience. But, it must be conceded, it was sometimes dangerous.

There was always the possibility of accident or injury, but this was a way of life. It was made only slightly more hazardous by the fact that no one else must know where the vision seeker was.

The real danger, however, was not from the elements or wild animals, but from the enemy. The Head Splitters were always a threat. Owl, the medicine man, had been captured during his vision quest and carried far away to be sold as a slave to strange tribes. True, in the end it had made his medicine even stronger, but it was certainly not a desirable thing.

And for a girl to take such risks was beyond the understanding of Long Walker. It was known that the Head Splitters loved to kidnap women or young girls of the People. "Our women are prettier than theirs" had long been the accepted attitude of the People.

It was true. Longer of limb and more graceful of movement, a girl of the People was a prize for a Head Splitter to capture.

For all these reasons Long Walker became increasingly apprehensive for Eagle Woman. He could see no way in which he could protect her from the mounting threats to her safety if she persisted in this course of action. That is, he could not protect her from herself.

He rose from his place of concealment, where he had been watching the girl's practice, and walked back toward the village. Angry and frustrated, Long Walker tossed a rock at a yapping dog that irritated him. The animal retreated with a yelp. If only all his worries could be banished so easily.

A young man on horseback was riding through the camp, calling an announcement. Long Walker hurried forward to listen.

The message was simple. The scouts had discovered a large herd of migrating buffalo moving into the greening area. The medicine man had burned last year's dry grass at the proper time, and the Moon of Greening had come with the returning herds.

There would be a great buffalo hunt tomorrow.

4

>> >> >>

Eagle Woman, tense with the excitement of the hunt, held her gray mare in line with the other hunters as they approached the top of the ridge. On her right Long Walker smiled a nervous smile of encouragement at the girl.

She knew he disapproved of her efforts. He had scarcely bothered to conceal that he had watched her every day at her practice. The knowledge affected the girl with mixed emotions. She was indignant that he should be so presumptuous, yet at the same time she was pleased. It was a good feeling to have a loyal friend such as Walker.

Eagle Woman tried constantly to reassure herself that this was the only basis for the warm sensation she felt when she thought about him. Of course she had no romantic interest in Long Walker. He was a friend, a good-natured competitor, whose company she enjoyed. Nothing more.

Besides, he had laughed at her. At the very memory, she gave her glossy braids a toss over her shoulder in indignation. At least Long Walker had had enough insight to refrain from repeating the error.

She looked straight ahead, a reassuring right hand resting on the neck of her horse. The animal had been a gift from her father. Cat quick, the mare was called Gray Cat by family and friends. It was descended directly from her grandfather's First Elk-dog, Lolita, and had much the same appearance and agility, it was said. Eagle had trained the little mare well, and confidence on the part of the girl had resulted in an effective team. The animal thoroughly understood the pursuit of the buffalo. There was no way to teach that. It would either be there or not.

The riders were now topping the grassy ridge, and Eagle Woman could see the dark shapes of numerous buffalo ahead. The mare's ears pricked sharply forward at the scent. Eagle Woman balanced carefully, alert lest the mare jump unexpectedly, but the animal remained calm.

On the left Long Elk, leader of the hunt, signaled forward, and the line moved at a faster walk. The scattered buffalo were becoming alert now. A nervous old cow lifted her head to catch the scent and moved uncertainly back and forth. Her vision was not acute enough to identify the approaching figures. Other animals, previously resting, were lumbering to their feet now, peering confusedly at the approaching hunters.

A shift in the light breeze suddenly allowed a whiff of human scent to drift in the direction of the herd, and an individual animal here and there started to trot away. Some merely stood and stared, still trying to visually identify the approaching line of hunters.

Long Elk kneed his horse forward, lance at ready, and the other hunters followed quickly. In the space of a few heartbeats the buffalo herd was running wildly, with the riders gaining rapidly.

Eagle Woman clutched her short bow and guided the horse forward with her knees, searching for a target. The gray mare, understanding the purpose of the exercise, pressed after the retreating buffalo, her ears flattened against her neck. They moved alongside a fat young cow, and the girl dropped the rein to the mare's neck, freeing both hands to shoot. She fitted an arrow to the string and pulled the bow to full draw, her eye on the soft flank just behind the rib cage. The bow twanged, and the feathered shaft, ranging forward into the chest, all but disappeared into the body of the running cow. The animal stumbled, and the horse and rider swept past.

Eagle Woman glanced to her right to see Long Walker make a well-aimed lance thrust at a large cow. She looked aside to find another target of her own. A yearling bull blundered past, and the girl's arrow again sought vital structures. The animal fell, bloody froth spewing from the nostrils, and the girl rode on.

An older bull snorted and threatened with a toss of his massive head as he brushed past. Eagle Woman refrained from loosing her arrow. The destructive might of a wounded bull was to be respected and avoided if possible. Besides, the girl told herself, the meat would be better on a fat young cow.

She called a warning to Long Walker and pointed to the aggressive herd bull. He reined aside and waved his thanks as the huge animal thundered past. A moment later Eagle Woman lost sight of her friend in the dust and confusion.

The herd was thinning now, the thunder of their myriad hooves fading into the distance. Eagle Woman glanced around to see the extent of the hunt's success. The short new grass of the meadow was strewn with dark bodies, some still moving or kicking feebly. Mounted hunters moved among the fallen buffalo, administering a final blow here and there. A thin haze of dust hung heavily over the scene.

The butchering party was straggling over the distant hill, and Eagle Woman turned to point out her kills to the members of her family. She wondered if she would be expected to help with the butchering, and the thought struck her as amusing. It had not occurred to her until now to wonder if she should perform the duties of both the hunter and the woman. Probably, she decided. It would do no harm and would give the others a good feeling.

A stray yearling cow came blundering up out of a rocky draw, panicky at being separated from the herd. The animal made a dash for open prairie, its route to pass close to Eagle Woman's position. The gray horse was instantly in pursuit, nearly unseating the rider.

Eagle Woman was still excited from the chase. The prospect of returning to the drudgery of butchering was not nearly so appealing as that of continuing the hunt. She leaned forward, fitting an arrow as she rode.

The cow doubled back, quick and evasive. This, the girl realized, was probably the reason for the animal's escape from the first onslaught. She reined the horse around and started pursuit again.

Other hunters, returning toward the area of the main kill, stopped to watch the chase. The sound of their hoots and laughter carried across the meadow, penetrating even the totally occupied thoughts of Eagle Woman.

It was a question, at the moment, whether embarrassment or anger was her uppermost emotion. She missed another run at her quarry, and a wave of laughter echoed from the spectators.

The girl was furious. There would be many warriors, she knew, who would delight in her failure. It would be only right, they would say smugly, that a woman who aspired to hunter and warrior status should be proved inept and incapable.

The cow dodged again, and the frustrated horse pivoted on its heels to pursue. Again Eagle Woman was almost unseated, but she held tightly with her knees. The inside of her thighs ached at the groin from the constant muscular strain.

Fiercely the girl calmed herself to reason how to

end the ludicrous scene. If the animal would only run straight away and allow her to pursue! But it had learned quickly that escape was effected by running straight, then turning back as the horse and rider approached.

The buffalo now stood still, facing the girl on the gray horse. The front legs were spread wide, sweating sides heaving from exertion. How simple it would be, thought Eagle Woman, if some of the other hunters would help her, would turn the running cow back for her. That would have been customary in the hunt. This, though, was a special circumstance. She knew she could expect no help. She must devise a means of success or be laughed at forever.

On the last turn the girl had noticed that the running buffalo usually feinted with a toss of the head and turned in the opposite direction. Perhaps she could take advantage of that fact. If she had a warning, even the space of a heartbeat, there might be time to loose an arrow. She rode slowly forward, and the cow blinked suspiciously, then turned to run.

The run was straight away, like previous sprints. Eagle Woman held tightly with her knees and let the finely trained horse approach on the animal's right side. She watched carefully for the telltale warning.

The signal came—the cow tossed her head left, then turned sharply across in front of the charging horse. Eagle Woman was already drawing her bow.

It was a difficult shot, impossible, almost. The girl concentrated on placing her arrow precisely as the brown blur of the moving form darted past. At the same time the horse had begun to drop to its haunches in a sliding pivot. Momentum carried the rider forward, over the horse's head, to crash heavily to the ground. Men rushed forward. The cow lay kicking, but the other form on the grass was still.

Slowly Eagle Woman began to move. Long Walker was first to reach her, cradling her head in his lap. A swelling purple bruise above the girl's left eye testified to the force of her fall. Dully she smiled at the young man.

Another hunter rode up and dismounted. "Well," he commented, "at least she made her kill!"

Long Walker had reached the height of his tension for the morning. He looked up indignantly at the speaker. "Stupid one!" he shouted. "This is her *third* kill! Did you make three kills today?"

5

» » »

It was thought by some that Eagle Woman, after her close encounter in the hunt, would not pursue the goal of becoming a member of a warrior society. Even though her three buffalo kills were admired, talked about, and praised, no one would have thought less of her had she let the matter drop. There were many who expected her to do so, and that would have been the end of it.

Long Walker knew better. He had helped the staggering girl back to her horse and assisted her in remounting. His heart was heavy. He had tried his utmost to avoid any action which would encourage this headstrong woman to pursue her ridiculous goal. The damage had been done, he realized, when he had laughed at her.

Now others had laughed at her, and she would never back down. Even though she had made three kills, more than anyone except Standing Bird, she would still feel the need to push ahead, to prove herself.

Long Walker viewed all this with a certain amount

of mixed feeling. He must admit, he had been thrilled with pride when he watched Eagle Woman skillfully drop the first two buffalo. He had been so busy admiring her dexterity, in fact, that he had made only one kill.

Actually he had not realized the true depth of his feeling until he saw her fall from the horse. As he lifted the limp form from the grass, full recognition of his feelings had swept over him. He felt close to this person as a friend, a rival, a competitor, yes, but there was the other hunger. He longed to hold her in his arms, as a man holds the woman he loves, to protect and comfort.

Long Walker had been able to hold the girl so for only a moment before she revived enough to resent it if he had continued. He had only the memory of the girl's body against him. The feeling was of soft and yielding curves, at the same time firm and muscular in total sensation. He had longed to continue to hold her, to minister to her injuries, and to tell her how much he admired her accomplishment in the hunt.

But he dared not. He wished not even to hint that he approved of this feat, because in truth he did not. He wished that Eagle Woman would behave more like a woman. Then he would know how he wished to respond. As things were, Long Walker began to feel that he should avoid contact with the girl. Any chance remark or action might drive them further apart, and he wished to avoid this at all cost.

The Elk-dog Society would be meeting a few suns later for one of the usual ceremonials. The Moon of Greening would progress to the Grass-growing Moon, and such a progression was traditionally observed by the warrior societies.

At any of these celebrations young warriors who had proven themselves in the hunt could request admission to the societies. It was at this time, Long Walker knew, that Eagle Woman would make her application. He had no doubt that she would be accepted, for the entire band admired her courage in the hunt.

It was the next step that the young man dreaded. The girl would be accepted as a provisional member, ready to undertake the vision quest. That in itself would be dangerous enough, but in proper order of events she would next be expected to participate in a major war party.

Of course she could refuse any of the steps and remain a lesser member of the warrior society. Long Walker knew her better than that. To do so would carry with it the implication of cowardice. Eagle Woman could never tolerate that. In fact, the young man knew, as she aspired to membership in the warrior society, striving for man things, she would require of herself that she not only equal, but better the efforts of the young men. It had been so in the buffalo hunt.

If there were only some way, Long Walker pondered, to stop her. His dilemma was that if he attempted to convince the girl, she would overreact in anger and be that much more difficult to deal with. If, on the other hand, he said nothing, he felt certain that Eagle Woman would begin the steps to full warrior status.

Aiee, what could be done? Discreetly he inquired as to the rules and customs involved. He sought out Standing Bird, leader of the Elk-dog Society, and explained his problem. The older man was sympathetic, carefully concealing his mild amusement over the situation.

"Yes, my son," he agreed, "it is a problem."

Under ordinary circumstances there would be no question as to the admission of qualified applicants. Their acceptance was a mere formality unless the applicant's qualifications were in doubt. In the case of Eagle Woman there would be no question. Her three kills were an outstanding record for a first hunt, far better than that of most.

"There is no doubt she is eligible," Standing Bird

continued. "She must be allowed to apply if she wishes."

"But, Uncle, there must be some way to stop her." Walker was almost pleading now.

Standing Bird shook his head. "No, I think not."

There was a long moment of silence, and the younger man started to turn away in dejection.

"Unless, of course," Standing Bird added with an amused smile, "you wish to use the Challenge."

Long Walker whirled to face his leader again. "The Challenge?"

"Yes. Any member of the Elk-dog Society may challenge the admission."

"What happens then?"

"A contest. The challenger must be able to prove the newcomer unfit."

Long Walker was becoming more interested. "And how is this done, Uncle?"

The older man was ready to regret having mentioned this possibility. Walker was serious in his wish to stop the girl.

"They compete with weapons, skill with Elk-dogs, anything." He finished with a vague wave of the hand, half hoping the young man would forget the whole thing.

"Who chooses the events?"

"The challenger first, then the new warrior, until one is clearly the winner."

Standing Bird was sorry he had even mentioned the possibility of the Challenge. It was used seldom, and usually only for spite. It could only lead to bad feelings and a potential split in the Elk-dog Society, perhaps in the band itself.

The young man was pondering the matter.

"Look, Walker," the older man spoke, still amused but becoming uneasy, "do not do this thing. It would only make the girl angry."

Long Walker was thinking precisely that. To use the Challenge would certainly stop the foolishness of the girl's becoming a warrior. He could defeat her in a number of the warrior skills. This would prevent her from undertaking the next steps. It could conceivably save her life.

But, on the other hand, it would drive her completely away from him. It could never be the same between them again. She would resent him to her dying day, and Long Walker would have defeated his own purpose. *Aiee*, what a choice! He could see no good coming from this, no matter what his actions.

He could let the girl proceed with her plans and allow her to risk her life in the aloneness of the vision quest, or later in combat.

Or he could try to stop her. If he did so, he would surely lose her anyway. Either way, she was lost to him, just when they had discovered each other and the joy of the time they spent together.

Long Walker's heart was very heavy.

6

>> >> >>

Long Walker need not have been so dejected. Eagle
Woman's thoughts and desires were much more nearly
like his own than he imagined.

When the girl had revived in Long Walker's arms,
her smile had been a reassurance that she was not
badly injured. Behind the smile, however, were deep
feelings that surprised even Eagle Woman. Through
the foggy mists of returning consciousness, she had
realized that she was glad to be in the arms of her
friend. Walker's nearness was reassuring and comforting in ways she had never experienced before.

She could easily have enjoyed remaining there for a
time, drawing strength and comfort from the young
warrior. There was also a certain pride in being the
object of Walker's concern and interest. But it must
end. Returning consciousness brought the awareness
of noise, dust, the returning hunters, and the beginning of the tasks of butchering.

Sweet Grass had insisted that the girl lie down in
the shade of the raised lodge cover. This was some-

thing of a relief for Eagle Woman. She had fully intended to assist her mother and the other women in the butchering, but she did not really feel equal to the task.

She lay in the shade, collecting her thoughts and trying to throw off the throbbing headache that had resulted from her fall. The swelling lump over her eye was tender to the touch, but it would heal in time. And she thought with a great deal of pride of her three kills. She smiled to herself. It was a good feeling to best the young men at their own skills.

More impressive than these sensations, however, were the new feelings and emotions revolving around her thoughts of Long Walker. The short moment she had lain in his arms had been so satisfying, so fulfilling. It was not so much a physical pleasure, she decided, though it was that, too. The important thing had been the sense of support, of his respect and approval. Of pride, even. She had sensed that Long Walker, in addition to his concern for her injuries, was proud and pleased by her accomplishment. And it was good to have him feel this way about her.

During the next few days Eagle Woman gradually established her plans. She saw little of Long Walker. She even suspected that he might be avoiding her, though she did not understand why. It might be that their moment of closeness had stirred new emotions in the breast of Long Walker, too. She smiled to herself at the thought, enjoying the feeling of warmth that the memory brought.

She would proceed with the plan to enter the warrior society, she had decided. She would probably even undertake her vision quest. Yes, that would be good. Then she would be an equal with the young men. She could accompany Long Walker on a war party or horse-stealing raid against the Head Splitters if she wished.

Or not, if she wished. It would give her the greatest possible choice. Her fantasies were extending to the coming years. That she and Walker would be together she had no doubt at all. The girl envisioned the two of them together through the future. They would hunt together, share in the management of their lodge. She would decide later about children. For now it was enough to dream of the companionship of Long Walker and the joy and friendship that they shared already.

She would, after the warrior ceremony, seek out her friend. They would talk and eventually would decide to marry. Eagle Woman was certain of that from the look she had seen in the eyes of Long Walker at the end of the hunt. She could hardly wait for the warrior ceremony.

The day came when the crier walked through the encampment of the Elk-dog band, shaking his rattles and calling out the announcement. The ceremony would be on the following evening, at the coming of darkness. Anyone could attend, and members of the other warrior societies, the Bowstrings and the Bloods, were invited to participate in a portion of the dance. There would be also, the young crier continued, the installation of novices who had proved themselves in the recent hunt.

Eagle Woman smiled, outwardly calm but excited inside. She hurried to reassure herself, for the hundredth time, that the garments she had chosen to wear were ready. Her fingers touched the soft buckskin, the carefully worked quill designs. Yes, everything was in order.

Finally, on the appointed day, Sun Boy carried his torch to the west, painted himself the ceremonial red, and retired to his lodge on the other side of the world. The People gathered in the center of the camp, where a fire was already burning. Several older men, who would serve as chanters and drum beaters, were tuning the great drum. Holding it near the fire, they warmed the skin to draw it taut and increase its resonance. Occasionally one of the aged warriors would tap on its surface with a dogwood drum stick, testing the tone.

Spectators were gathering, and the dancers assisted each other in last-moment adjustments to their garments and facial paint. Eagle Woman approached quietly and took her place at the edge of the circle with two young men who were requesting admission.

A low murmur of conversation rippled around the crowd. Eagle Woman had not worn her warrior-sister dress, but the shirt and leggings of a man! Apparently there were many who had not heard of her intentions.

One of the other warrior sisters waved and smiled encouragingly to her, and Eagle Woman seated herself beside the young men. The dance was about to begin.

There was less formality about this celebration of the hunt than that at the ritual Sun Dance or even the annual Warriors' Dance. Still, there were customs to observe. There were open dances, where all joined in the enjoyment and the singing. Then there were songs and reenactments of great or well-remembered hunts.

Eagle Woman participated at the appropriate times, stepping around the circle in time to the rhythm of the big drum. It seemed strange to see the other warrior sisters in their roles as priestesses. Hers was now a new role, and in a way the girl regretted the feeling of that which had been.

She saw Long Walker across the circle, and she nodded and smiled. Walker smiled back, but his expression was disappointing. There was a certain reserve, not the previous closeness they had shared. Eagle Woman knew that it was because he disapproved of her warrior aspirations.

No matter, she smiled to herself. She could prevail on him. Soon she could take him aside and tell him, simply as a friend, of course, that this was the end of it. Only the vision quest and she would be ready to withdraw from further warriorlike ambitions.

Except for enjoyment, of course. She felt that she would be pleased, riding with Long Walker, sharing the excitement and danger of the hunt. They could be a very effective hunting team, she knew, with their respective skills. She would seek him out immediately after the dance, to talk and to share her ideas. It would be good to be with him again.

At last the crier was announcing the aspiring applicants to the Elk-dog Society, describing their deeds in the recent hunt. Eagle Woman stood self-consciously with the two young men and listened. One had made a good run with the lance, the other a double kill with the bow. The latter was a powerful young man who carried a very heavy bow. Several witnesses had seen his arrow thrust entirely through a galloping cow to kill her calf running on the other side. *Aiee*, this was powerful medicine!

Yet even this event was overshadowed by the fact that Eagle Woman had secured three animals at great risk to herself. There were exclamations of approval around the circle. The successful kill of three for a novice was greatly admired—even more so, to be sure, when the hunter involved was a woman. Capable women were highly prized among the People.

Now it remained only to announce the formal admission of the applicants. The murmurs of approval had hardly died before the shocking event of the evening occurred. A young warrior was rising to his feet to signal for recognition.

"My brothers!" he shouted.

Most of the spectators recognized the young man as Long Walker, friend of the girl, Eagle Woman. No doubt he wished to make a speech of praise and approval. Everyone settled back, pleased and happy for the young people.

Eagle Woman could hardly contain herself. How thoughtful for Walker to do this for her. Her heart swelled with pride as she waited for the crowd to quiet for the young man's speech.

"My brothers!" Long Walker shouted again for attention.

All eyes were now fixed on the handsome youth as he turned to Standing Bird, leader of the Society. "My chief," he spoke firmly, "I claim the right of the Challenge!"

7
>> >> >>

Eagle Woman was furious. The entire encampment was aware of her wrath.

There had been a gasp from the onlookers as Long Walker made his formal statement. No one could remember the last time the Challenge had been used. Many did not even know the meaning. Even Eagle Woman was not certain.

She felt that she had been betrayed. At the height of her triumph, her achievement had been destroyed. Worst of all, it had been done by her friend. Surely it could never be the same. She could never again feel toward Walker as she had come to feel in the past few moons. He had destroyed their closeness.

It had been announced by Standing Bird that the Challenge would take place on the following day, with the agreement of the two principals involved. Both had nodded assent, and the induction of the other aspiring warriors had proceeded. Eagle Woman stood, embarrassed, shamed, alone, smoldering with anger.

She understood only vaguely the use of the Challenge. She would be expected to compete in warrior skills, but beyond that she knew very little. It seemed an eternity until the ceremonies were over and she could leave the area. There were many who had spoken to her with words of encouragement and confidence.

Long Walker avoided her as the People dispersed into the night to return to their own lodges. She was furious, but also disappointed. How differently the evening had ended from the way she had planned. She had envisioned a warm congratulation from her friend, then a quiet walk along the river in the pleasant moonlight. She would have told him of her plans, and there might have been a soft embrace. Now it was gone, destroyed. She saw the young man slipping away and hurried after him.

"Walker!" she called.

Unable to escape without a loss of dignity, Long Walker stopped and turned to meet the onslaught of the irate girl. Her anger rose like a flash flood in a prairie stream as she strode toward him. By the time she faced him, Eagle Woman's wrath was ready to overflow its banks.

"What are you doing?" She almost shouted at him. Then, not waiting for an answer, the girl continued.

"Walker, you know I have met the requirements. I have made my buffalo kills. I have as much right in the Elk-dog Society as you!" Her voice became shrill and tight, rising in pitch with her emotions.

"What are you trying to do to me?"

For the first time since the tirade began, she paused long enough for Long Walker to answer. Even so, he was not ready. There was a long moment while he attempted to clear the lump in his throat. He saw the sparkle of tears on her cheeks in the moonlight, tears of sheer frustration.

"Why, Walker, why?" she insisted.

The young man gulped again and finally found words. "Because. Someone has to save you from yourself."

"Son of a snake," she spat at him, "you will have to

save yourself from me! I will beat you at the Challenge!"

She whirled and stalked away, leaving the dejected young man alone in the moonlight. *Aiee*, he thought, the world is turning to dung. Sadly he turned toward the river, to walk and to think.

Eagle Woman sought out her father back at their own lodge. She must find out exactly what the Challenge implied.

"It is a series of contests," Eagle explained. "He will choose one, then you. There may be two, or several more, until one or the other is clearly the winner."

"He chooses the first?"

"Yes, then you choose."

She knew what the first choice of Long Walker would be. He had always been adept with the lance. Eagle Woman had learned its use but had never preferred the weapon. It was too heavy and cumbersome. She had concentrated on the bow. Ah, that would be her choice when the time came. She sought her robes, knowing full well she would sleep little this night. In her smoldering anger she hoped that Long Walker would sleep poorly, too.

Sun Boy rose and lighted his torch, and its rays shone down on the camp of the People. They were stirring early this day, the area buzzing with excitement.

Standing Bird, as leader of the Elk-dog Society, would be in charge of the contests. The challenger had chosen the lance as the first trial, and young men were scattered up the slope to the top of the hill placing the target hoops.

These circles of willow were a hand's span in diameter, hung from the twigs of the sumac or dogwood which dotted the slope. The horsemen would charge up the hill, threading on the lance as many targets as possible. The one bringing more rings back to the starting point would be the winner.

Eagle Woman placed her saddle pad on Gray Cat

and tightened the girth. She felt that there was a good chance that she might be able to compete at this. Gray Cat was quick and agile and could maneuver well on the tricky footing of the slope.

The girl swung to the mare's back, and Bobcat handed her a lance. He gave an encouraging smile. Eagle Woman wished that her brother would take this contest more seriously. He was being helpful, but his mischievous glance said that he thought the entire matter somewhat amusing.

Standing Bird was speaking now, holding a fist-sized stone at arm's length. "When the stone drops, begin!"

Eagle Woman glanced over at Long Walker, who was just swinging to his horse's back. They had not spoken this morning. There was a hard knot in her stomach, a sour taste in her mouth. This was all wrong. The two should be riding off together as friends.

Walker's horse bolted forward, and the girl realized that Standing Bird had dropped the signal stone. She had been preoccupied with her thoughts. Cursing silently, she dug heels into the startled mare's flanks, and the animal leaped after the other horse.

Long Walker had already threaded the first target and raised his lance point. The ring slid down the weapon's shaft, and he caught it with his right hand, lowering the point again as he approached the next hoop.

Frantically Eagle Woman pursued. She must reach some of the targets before the other horseman. So far she had not even had an opportunity to try for a score.

She glanced ahead. Some of the young men had fanned out to the left, and she saw the white rings of peeled willow against green foliage in that direction, too. She reined the mare to the left. She must ignore Walker's successes and concentrate on her own. The lance neatly passed through the first ring, and she kneed the horse toward the next.

By this time the animal had realized the purpose of the game. Quick as a heartbeat, the well-trained mare changed flying front feet and shifted the angle of mo-

tion toward the next hoop. It was hanging at a difficult angle, but the girl skillfully centered the target
and slid it up to join the others. She wondered how
Long Walker was doing but dared not stop to look.

The next target was easy, and the next also. She
paused to glance over at Long Walker, while the mare
scrambled over a rocky ledge toward a nearby clump
of sumac with white target rings in evidence. She
speared another, and as she lifted the lance she realized how tired her right arm was becoming. The weapon
was growing heavier with each motion, and it seemed
she could not hold it steady while she concentrated
on the white hoop ahead. Still she managed to lift the
point at the last moment to enter the dangling ring.

There were no more targets above her now, and she
swung back toward where Long Walker had zigzagged
up the slope. One ring still hung on a scrubby bush
between them, and she kicked the gray mare forward.
She was nearer the target, but the other saw it at
almost the same moment.

Eagle Woman lunged forward, readying the lance.
Her shoulder muscles ached from the exertion, her
right arm seemed wooden from the elbow down. If she
could only lift the lance point to impale this one last
target. It had become symbolic of the contest.

The girl gritted her teeth and tried to ignore the
pain of aching muscles as she concentrated on the
run. Carefully she bore down on the target ring, moved
the point of the weapon slightly for greater accuracy,
and rushed past the bush. To her consternation there
was no white willow loop hanging on the lance shaft
as she raised it. She had missed.

She wheeled the horse for another run, trying to
ignore the drumming of hooves behind her. Walker's
horse was gaining, but she saw that she would reach
the target first.

She had lifted the lance upright, but she now lowered the point for another run. This time she would
not miss. A new surge of determination gave her momentum, and the lance sped straight toward the ring.

Eagle Woman was never sure later whether Walker's next action was deliberate or not. She never asked him. For now she only knew that Gray Cat stumbled, scrambled for footing, and swept past the target out of reach. At the same moment the girl realized the reason for the stumble. The gray mare had been jostled aside by the larger horse.

Long Walker, now almost at leisure, speared the dangling ring and turned his horse at a walk to the starting point. The crowd was cheering, and people were already beginning to pay off side bets.

Furious and frustrated, Eagle Woman followed. She elected to say nothing about the jostling.

The two drew their horses up before the waiting Standing Bird, and the girl let her lance point touch the ground. Six willow hoops rattled down the shaft to bounce against each other at the tip.

Long Walker did likewise. Glumly Eagle Woman counted the rattling wooden rings. Seven, eight, nine! Her anger burned with even more resentment.

There had been only fifteen targets on the hillside. Long Walker had not even needed the last ring, the one he had jostled her aside to reach. He had already won.

8
>> >> >>

Eagle Woman was not concerned with her ability to best the challenger at the next event. She was confident that her ability with the bow was superior. When she announced her choice for the contest, the expression on Long Walker's face said that he believed so, too. The girl had always bested him in the use of this weapon.

Though she was confident, Eagle Woman looked farther ahead and despaired. A win with the bow would only bring the contestants even again, and the next choice was Long Walker's. *Aiee*, there were many things at which he excelled. Which would he choose? Even so, she must take one step at a time. The first was the trial with bow and arrows.

This test would be on foot. Already two young men were placing the stuffed-skin target at a distance of fifty paces. In the center of its surface, Standing Bird had painted a black spot the size of a hand's span. Each of the contestants would use three arrows, shooting alternately. If there was no clear winner, they would continue to shoot in turn until Standing Bird declared the contest at an end.

Eagle Woman stepped to the line and assumed the bowman's stance. The dull-brown target seemed very small at this distance. She could hardly see the black center at all. She had sorted through her arrows, choosing the best and straightest, those with perfect balance. One, which initially appeared superior, was rejected because of a bulky and uneven lashing where the feathers were tied with sinew.

The girl fitted the first shaft to the bowstring and drew the arrow to its head. The release felt satisfactory, and the missile was on its way. A shout went up from the group of spectators near the target, and one of the young men signaled the result. The feathered shaft was a hand's span to the right of the black center.

Irritated, Eagle Woman stepped back. She must allow more carefully for the wind. The light breeze from the south was pushing gently at the flying arrow, bending its course a trifle to the north.

Long Walker, with the advantage of having observed the initial shot, stepped confidently forward. Also, his stronger bow would throw the arrow faster, causing less deflection by the wind. Eagle Woman watched closely. Perhaps he would overcorrect.

Apparently this was exactly what happened. Long Walker's confidence seemed shattered as the result was shouted back. His arrow rested a hand's span left of the mark.

Eagle Woman stepped forward again. She had studied the wind as it stirred the grasses to the left of the target. The breeze was light and shifting, at times almost dying. She could use these observations. It was a matter of timing.

Carefully she watched, waiting until the ripple of the grass was stilled for a few heartbeats. Then, at the precisely proper moment, the girl drew and released her arrow. The release was smooth, and she knew before the shaft struck that it had flown true. Again a cheer went up from the observers. The feathered end protruded from the black spot.

Long Walker's next arrow went wild, nearly missing the skin target altogether. Such things happened. A slightly imperfect shaft, a defective feather, a puff of breeze, or perhaps even a poor release. Some of the spectators jumped in mock alarm and moved back from the area of the target. Long Walker smiled good-naturedly and waved to the laughing crowd.

The girl readied her last arrow. The contest was as good as won now. If she could hit the skin at all, Walker must place his arrow in the black center to even equal her effort.

Perhaps she was overconfident, not paying enough attention to the breeze. It would be easy to blame a defective arrow. Whatever the reason, Eagle Woman knew at the moment of release that her contest was in trouble. Helpless, she watched the misguided shaft fly with agonizing slowness across the flat of the meadow. Missing the grass-stuffed target entirely, the arrow struck the ground beyond, bounced, and leaped to shatter itself against the stony outcrop on the hillside.

A subdued moan came from the spectators, with an occasional joyful chuckle from those who had bets on Long Walker. Now the day had suddenly turned.

Long Walker now had only to hit the skin target to win. Amused, smiling, the young man stepped to the line and carefully readied his arrow.

Why doesn't he go ahead, the dejected Eagle Woman fumed. He had won, had proved his contention. Now he had only to shoot, to finish the contest. She would be relieved, actually, to have the thing over, to return to normal living. Unfortunately that could never really happen. Her life could never be the same again. Worst of all, her friendship with Long Walker had been shattered, leaving a puzzling sense of emptiness and loss.

The girl wished to turn away, to leave the scene of the contest, but pride held her. She must watch Long

Walker make his last shot, and then it would be over. The young man drew the arrow to its flint point, and the string twanged as he released his hold. The arrow sped on its way, and Eagle Woman started to turn away with a heavy heart.

Suddenly there were shouts of shocked surprise from the group of spectators near the target. Eagle Woman turned quickly, in time to see Walker's arrow skipping and bouncing on the hillside. Long Walker had missed!

The surprised shouts blended into a sort of cheer from the supporters of Eagle Woman. Disgruntled losers at wagering were glumly beginning to pay off their bets before the girl realized the importance of this last shot. Her first two shots had been better than Walker's, and both had missed on the third. She had won the contest.

Close on the heels of the thought came another. Surely Long Walker could have easily hit the skin target if he had wished. Was it possible that he had intentionally missed to allow her to save face?

The thought became a worrisome thing. If it were true, Eagle Woman did not know whether to love or hate him for it.

In actual fact, however, she was never to know whether the miss was intentional or not.

9

>> >> >>

Sun Boy was high overhead as Long Walker chose the next challenge. The crowd of spectators had been growing all morning as word spread of the excitement of the contest.

"I choose the hunt!"

Standing Bird nodded in agreement.

"It is good. Both will ride out, and see who makes the first kill."

He gestured toward the distant prairie, with scattered buffalo dotting the bright green of the grassland.

"What of the rules?" Eagle Woman demanded. "Must it be a buffalo?"

"Did you wish to try for a rabbit, Eagle Woman?" someone called.

The crowd laughed, and Standing Bird held up his hand for silence.

"Buffalo, elk, deer, antelope," he said seriously. "Any of these."

"How will it be known who is first? We may be out of sight."

Again, Standing Bird considered for a moment.

"I will be at this spot," he indicated. "You will bring me an ear from your kill. The first to return with the ear has won."

He looked around. The observers were eagerly awaiting this next contest. Wagering was heavy.

"Now, no one is to follow them," he warned. "Their hunt must not be disturbed."

Eagle Woman was thinking rapidly as she tightened the girth on the gray mare. There were two contests, almost. The hunt must be successful, but the race back to Standing Bird with the proof would be equally important.

Her kill, then, should be as close to camp as possible. A brief chase, or none at all. Anything to keep the return distance as short as possible, to be the first to arrive.

The two contestants rode out together, side by side, in the direction of the scattered buffalo. They did not speak. Eagle Woman longed to break the uncomfortable silence but was reluctant to do so. It would be pleasant to discuss the hunt, the weather, anything, but Long Walker rode in silence, looking straight ahead. His mouth was set in a determined line which precluded conversation.

How had it happened so suddenly, the girl wondered. Only a few suns ago the two had shared their thoughts, goals, and dreams. Now it was gone. They had come to a parting of the way.

As she pondered these thoughts, Eagle Woman noticed a shifting movement to the left. Changing patterns of light and shadow in a small canyon told of grazing animals. She glanced at Long Walker, but his attention was fixed on the buffalo in the open prairie ahead.

Of course. He would use the lance. He must have an open area for pursuit to make his kill. Eagle Woman, on the other hand, could function well in a more broken area. She could use the bow either in close pursuit or at a distance. She was certain that Long

Walker had envisioned this hunt as an all-out charge into the herd, the hunters riding alongside a galloping buffalo to make the kill. But with the bow as her weapon, there were other options. She could approach quietly, without disturbing the grazing quarry. She could even stalk on foot.

Ah! This thought had not occurred until now. Another glance at the small canyon revealed trees, brush, and rocky, uneven slopes. A perfect place for a stalk. Long Walker was paying no attention to the canyon since it was unsuitable for his purposes. The girl reined her horse aside.

"Good hunting, Walker!"

The young man looked across at her, surprised at the break in the silence.

"Yes," he stammered finally. "You, also." He rode straight ahead.

Eagle Woman's gray mare tried for a moment to follow the other horse. The animal had sensed that a hunt was at hand and was becoming excited at the prospect of the chase.

This did not follow the girl's plan. The horse must remain calm. Firmly she drew the rein, and the reluctant Gray Cat turned aside. The animal was still nervous and skittish, and Eagle Woman headed for a small clump of trees, near the mouth of the canyon but out of sight from within.

She swung down, tied the gray to a tree, and, as a precaution, knotted a thong around the mare's nose to prevent the animal from calling out. Taking her bow and two arrows, she slipped quietly toward the broken slope of the canyon's mouth. Long Walker was already out of sight around the shoulder of the hill.

Eagle Woman moved quickly along an obscure game trail which threaded among the dogwood and sumac on the slope. She paused behind a boulder to view the scene and to plan her approach.

There were five animals in sight, two cows with calves and a yearling bull, the latter probably the last season's calf of the nearer cow. Eagle Woman carefully evaluated the possibilities. One cow was lying down, rechewing its food, while the other stood nearby doing likewise. The young bull was standing aimlessly near the others, lazy and a trifle sleepy in appearance. That would be her quarry, the girl decided. The bull would not be quite so wary and experienced.

The breeze was right, from the animals toward her, so they would not catch her scent. A clump of sumac presented excellent concealment within easy bow shot. There would be only a short stalk through open grass to reach the brushy clump. But she must move quickly. Had Long Walker started his run yet? She wondered as she dropped to a crouch and moved forward, gripping her weapon.

It was an easy approach at first. The resting animals appeared relaxed, not noticing the slim figure slipping among the rocks and brush. Quickly, though, came the last cluster of broken rocks. She must begin her crawl across the open.

All her skill in crawling close to the earth was called into use. As quickly as was practical, the girl slithered forward, using each sparse clump of realgrass for concealment. The distance she must crawl was no more than fifty paces, yet three times she saw the wary old cows become restless and start to swing their heads curiously. Each time she froze, motionless, until the animals resumed their chewing. The last time she stopped Eagle Woman thought the buffalo would never quiet. One cow paced restlessly, stopping frequently to gaze in the direction of the stalker.

The girl had been caught in an extremely awkward posture, one knee forward and at a cramped angle. She braced herself with suffering muscles, afraid to do more than blink an eye. An ant crawled slowly up a grass blade not a hand's span in front of her eyes. It felt as though another was doing the same across her left ankle. Carefully Eagle Woman disciplined her actions. If the insect decided to bite, she must not jump or move involuntarily. She knew that the buffalo's vision was poor and that if she only remained motionless, she would not likely be seen.

At last the suspicious cow appeared to accept that nothing was amiss. Sleepily the animal returned to chewing.

Eagle Woman slid forward, now in the concealment of the sumac clump. She peered between the stems, fitting an arrow to her bowstring. The young bull stood broadside, chewing contentedly.

She must place her arrow carefully. An animal pierced through the heart might panic and run wildly as it died. She would try for the lungs. The bull faced slightly away from her, exposing the left flank. Eagle Woman drew her arrow to the head and smoothly released the string.

For a moment it appeared that she had missed. There was only a slight flinch, and the bull swung his tail as he might at the bite of a fly. Slowly the animal's knees buckled, and he began to sag ponderously to the ground, bloody froth spewing from the nostrils.

Eagle Woman sprang from concealment, sprinting forward while she fumbled at her waist for her flint knife. She did not find it immediately and glanced down as she halted near the dying buffalo and reached for the ear.

Panic seized her as the truth finally sank home. The knife was gone, lost somewhere in the tall grass as she had crept forward on her belly. Frantically she turned to search for it, but she quickly realized the futility. Time was critical. She might still be searching when Long Walker had returned with his trophy.

Be calm, she told herself. Think, reason, decide what to do. There must be some way to sever the ear. She glanced around for a sharp stone, knowing that there would be none. Her eyes fell upon her bow and the remaining arrow, where she had laid the weapon on the grass. Of course!

Hardly had the thought formed before she had seized the arrow and was using the point as a knife, sawing through skin and cartilage. She finished the cut, jerked the ear free, and sprinted toward her horse.

The girl jerked the thong loose, untied the mare, and started to swing up, but she was hampered. Her left hand held her bow and arrows, the right the precious ear which symbolized the contest. She seemed not to have enough hands. Without hesitation she grasped the hairy trophy in her teeth and vaulted to the horse's back, drumming heels into the mare's sides.

They shot from the clump of trees, and the mare sprinted toward the camp. The girl was dimly aware of hooves drumming behind her but did not even look back. She brought the mare to a sliding stop before the knot of cheering onlookers. Standing Bird stood smiling and extended his hand to receive the symbol of proof.

Eagle Woman spat out the furry ear and handed it to the Elk-dog chief, just as Long Walker's horse slid to a stop behind her.

"Eagle Woman," chuckled Standing Bird, "there is blood on your face."

10

>> >> >>

It was near day's end, and Long Elk announced that no further contest would start. The Challenge would resume in the morning, with Eagle Woman choosing the contest.

Meanwhile both hunters returned to the scene of their kills to guide the butchering parties. There would be little time to salvage the meat before darkness fell. By morning, coyotes and other predators of the night would have left little of use.

Eagle Woman would retrieve the arrow which had made such an all-important kill. In addition, she wished to search for her knife.

Carefully, time after time, she retraced the path of her stalk, looking for any sign, but without success. Shadows were growing long, and the others were straggling back to camp, laden with meat, before the girl conceded that the knife was gone. She regretted the loss, but weapons were sometimes lost or broken. It could be replaced. Her main regret was an irritation with herself for her carelessness.

Eagle Woman had already stated that tomorrow's contest would be a race. A horse race, a match between the two contestants to show their ability in handling the Elk-dog. The girl counted on the speed and agility of Gray Cat against the more ponderous strength of Long Walker's big bay. In addition, she counted some advantage in the fact that her own weight was much less for a horse to carry than that of Long Walker.

Eagle Woman found it difficult to sleep that night, even in her state of physical exhaustion. There was far too much excitement in the air. The People were enjoying the contest of the Challenge immensely. There had not been such a time of interest since the Sun Dance and the Big Council. The stories of the contested events of the day were being told and retold over the evening fires. Interest in tomorrow's race was high, and the stakes in the wagering were becoming heavy. Bobcat had returned to the lodge to relate that one man had wagered his best buffalo horse against his friend's bow and a new buckskin shirt with extraordinarily fine quill work.

Bobcat was amused, but Eagle Woman had mixed feelings. It was flattering to have people express confidence in her, but also irritating that they would argue and make bets over the turning points in her life.

Her basic feeling, however, as she lay in her robes waiting for sleep to come, was one of confidence. Of the three contests so far, she had won two. If she could win the race tomorrow, Long Walker would probably concede, and her admission to the Elk-dog Society would be accepted. From her present winning position it was becoming easier to forgive Walker for the Challenge. Possibly their relationship could be restored after all. Having proved herself, she would be ready to forgive and forget, and surely Long Walker would do the same. With this pleasant fantasy skipping playfully through her mind, she finally fell asleep.

It seemed only a moment later that she awoke. The

rising sun streamed through the doorway of the lodge, and she heard the busy noises of the camp as the People came awake to begin the day. Children called out, dogs barked, a horse whinnied beside its owner's lodge.

At the sound of the horse, Eagle Woman was wide awake. This was the day of the race, the deciding event of the Challenge. Quickly she rose, pulled the hunting shirt over her head, and stepped into her leggings.

There was meat at the fire, and though she did not feel hungry, she ate a little. She would need strength today. Her parents wished her well, and they all emerged from the lodge to face the day and the contest.

Eagle Woman went to bring her horse, and led at a walk toward the area Standing Bird had designated. A crowd had already gathered, and there was a happy air of excitement as the People discussed, argued, wagered, or called to latecomers to hurry.

Long Walker was already present, his big bay stallion dancing excitedly, recognizing a race or hunt of some sort. The gray mare, too, was prancing and side-stepping in anticipation.

Eagle Woman had decided not to use the bulky grass-filled saddle pad for the race. She had tied a simple rawhide girth around the animal's chest and withers. This would suffice to hold to, and for practical purposes she would be riding bareback and unencumbered.

Standing Bird was pointing out the course. "You will ride around the tree at the top of the hill, across to the two together there at the edge of the meadow, and back here."

The riders nodded, mentally studying the terrain. It was good, Eagle Woman saw. The first leg of the course was slightly uphill, the turn fairly level. The two trees at the meadow's edge presented no problem, but the final stretch of the race would be along the low-lying flat next to the stream. That area, she recalled, had several spots that were soft and boggy. It would be necessary to avoid places with poor footing.

Now Standing Bird was holding a stone at arm's length. "Are you ready?"

Both riders nodded, and almost immediately the stone dropped.

Gray Cat leaped forward, true to her name, and had taken a lead before the larger horse gathered himself to spring. Eagle Woman clung to the rawhide girth and urged the mare forward with her heels.

Behind her came the shouts of the spectators and the drumming of hooves. She could hear Long Walker's big bay gaining, drawing closer. Then the stallion's head came into the corner of her vision, beside her right knee.

The animal's nostrils were flared, ears flattened, and with every stride the bay drew forward. Now even, now ahead, and Eagle Woman was looking at the massive driving muscles of the stallion's hind quarters.

The first tree loomed ahead, and the bay stallion swung wide around it, Long Walker fighting to turn the animal. This was what Eagle Woman had hoped for. Quickly she kneed the gray mare close to the tree, turning sharply, pivoting inside the arc of the larger animal's turn.

The girl drummed heels into the mare's flanks and sprinted toward the second turn, the two trees. Again the bay stallion came from behind with his longer stride, passing the gray to reach the turning point first. Long Walker had better control now, and the stallion did not lose so much ground on the turn. The two started to press for the final stretch at almost the same instant, neck and neck.

Eagle Woman's heart sank as the bay started to pull ahead. She saw no way her smaller mare could make up the lost distance.

Then the big stallion began to strike the heavy going in the low area near the stream. Great chunks of mud flew high in the air as the animal lunged forward, fighting the sticky soil with every stride. Eagle

Woman had the advantage of seeing where the other horse had struck soft footing, and now she pulled slightly to the left, away from the stream. As the stallion floundered and struggled in the uneven turf, the gray swept past and into the lead.

To Long Walker's credit, he did assess the situation rapidly and correct his course, but it was too late. There was no way in which he could now overtake the sprinting Gray Cat. The animals swept across the finish line only a stride apart, and Eagle Woman had won.

The crowd was cheering wildly, and the girl turned her sweating horse to trot back toward where Standing Bird waited. Surely, now, the Challenge was over. She had won at three of the four contests. Walker would concede, and they would be friends again.

Smiling, she faced the young man as the two drew up before the Elk-dog leader. To her surprise, Long Walker's face was dark with anger. His expression said clearly that he was not ready to quit.

"The next contest," Walker snapped irritably, "is *mine!*"

11

>> >> >>

Standing Bird was becoming uneasy about the progress of this Challenge. At the present stage of events, one of the adversaries should be ready to concede, but there was no sign of weakening on the part of either. Here were two proud and stubborn young people, neither willing to relinquish a principle. *Aiee*, it was a worrisome thing.

Eagle Woman had bested her challenger in the past three contests, but the next was to be of Long Walker's choosing—and he was angry now. He was practically shouting at the girl.

"You think it is amusing to do the things warriors do, as a game. I tell you, Eagle Woman, it is not that way. As a warrior, you must prepare for hand combat. Can you do that?" Without waiting for an answer, he hurried on. "The next contest will answer. We will wrestle."

There was a hoot of derision from somewhere in the rear, and Walker jerked his head around sharply. He was met by silence. There was none in the crowd who dared openly to criticize so able a man as Long Walker. It would be a matter of quiet chuckles and obscene jokes in private.

"It is good," announced Standing Bird, feeling full well that it was not. "You will use no knives or other weapons. You will fight until one is held helpless."

The horses were led away, and an area of smooth, level ground was chosen, swiftly ringed by the crowd. Betting was slow. There were few who believed that the slim girl would be skilled enough to prevail against the strength of Long Walker.

The contestants circled, warily looking for an opening. There were several feints and quick withdrawals, neither combatant attaining a grasp. The onlookers began to cry for action.

Long Walker, seeing an opportunity, rushed forward to grapple, but the girl was quick. She pivoted, seized an outstretched arm, and used the momentum of the young man's rush to effect the ancient hip throw. Walker landed heavily flat on his back, stunned and out of breath.

Eagle Woman circled, waiting, while the crowd howled with laughter. She was attempting, at all costs, to avoid the grappling that would depend on sheer strength. Her only chance was to use skill and finesse.

Long Walker rose slowly, burning with anger, and rushed again. Once more the girl avoided him, this time by skipping nimbly aside.

By the third rush Walker's mood had steadied, and he was thinking more sensibly. He feinted, then grasped, and the two grappled to roll on the ground.

It seemed only a heartbeat's time to Eagle Woman until she found herself pinned on her back. Her opponent held both her wrists firmly, and she felt his weight on her outstretched body. Both were breathing heavily. Her vision was blurred, and she heard only dimly the shouts of the crowd. In her left ear she could feel the hot panting breath of Long Walker. She stopped struggling for a moment.

Here was a new and exciting sensation, something

foreign to her experience. The pressure of Walker's muscular chest, flattening her breasts against her ribs, was not completely unpleasant. She was acutely aware of the weight of his body on her hips and thighs. *Aiee*, she felt, rather than thought, why not give it up? She longed to simply relax and wished to think more about this new sensation which had startled her.

The next moment Eagle Woman was furious with herself—furious, ashamed, and embarrassed that she should even have such thoughts before a crowd of gawking spectators.

She sank her teeth into Long Walker's neck near the shoulder and kneed him in the groin. As Walker grunted in pain and surprise, she took advantage of his loosened grip to pull her arms loose. They rolled over and over, the girl biting, kicking, gouging, scratching, ultimately pulling free to spring to her feet. The crowd shouted with delight.

Eagle Woman had no delusions. There would appear to be no way she could pinion the stronger warrior to win this contest. Eventually Long Walker would break free.

He was rising, now, to hands and knees, breathing heavily, hurting. Blood trickled from his neck and from scratches on his face. The girl circled, panting and exhausted, fighting the impulse to run to him and minister to his injuries. Long Walker rose to his feet, swaying, teeth clenched against the pain in his belly, to make another rush.

This time Eagle Woman was unable to evade his grasp. He seized a wrist, whirled her around to grasp her hair, and they tumbled again into the dust.

The girl fought ineffectively as her strength ebbed, and he pushed her, face down, against the ground. He sat astride her and held her tightly until her struggles ceased.

Somehow there was little triumph in the face of Long Walker as he rose. Eagle Woman rolled over and sat up, spitting dirt and grass from her mouth. She was completely exhausted and would gladly have concluded the entire Challenge then and there except that it was now impossible.

Because, she recalled wearily, she was still ahead. She could not concede while she was winning, even if she wished. The contests must go on. How long would it be until Long Walker conceded her right to warrior status? Or, she thought gloomily, until she was beaten badly enough to be able to concede with dignity? She looked for Long Walker to see if he appeared ready to give up.

The young man had gone down to the stream's edge, followed by some of his supporters and young admirers. He was on his knees in the shallows, pouring water over his head and shoulders.

"Eagle Woman," called Standing Bird, "the next choice is yours. What shall it be?"

The girl had been looking at the stream, longing to immerse her tired, hot, dirty, and sore body in its cooling waters. Without even looking around she answered immediately. "Swimming!"

12
≫ ≫ ≫

The People straggled upstream, the distance of a long bow shot, to the swimming place. By tradition the tribe loved water when it was available. Swimming, for skill as well as enjoyment, was a major activity of the Rabbit Society. Whenever possible the People camped near a stream usable for swimming.

The streams that meander across the rolling prairie twist and turn to form loops and arcs and deep, clear pools beneath rocky ledges. It was to one of these favorite swimming places that the group now moved.

Standing Bird sent two youngsters splashing across the stream to a ledge a stone's throw from where they stood. They placed two willow sticks, as thick as one's finger and a hand's span in length, on the flat stone shelf. The competitors would race to retrieve a stick and return it to the hand of Standing Bird.

Eagle Woman, now breathing more easily, was gaining in confidence. As a child she had been easily the best swimmer in the Rabbit Society. It was said that the girl could swim like an otter. Many times during their early years she had defeated Long Walker.

Bobcat placed his hand affectionately on his sister's arm. "This contest is yours, Eagle Woman. You are like a fish in the water. Show them!"

Heavy betting had resumed, for the People knew quite well that this was an area of skill for Eagle Woman. Larger bets were made now on the total outcome of the Challenge. The girl was still ahead in the contests, and this was conceded by most to be her best opportunity.

She glanced over at Long Walker. He had discarded his hunting shirt, and she could plainly see the injury she had inflicted on his neck. Her fury had cooled now, and she felt a sympathy for her friend and a slight regret for having hurt him. *Aiee,* how had they become involved in this stupid contest? She would be so happy when it was over and they could return to a normal relationship. If, indeed, that could ever be.

Eagle Woman was almost preoccupied with her thoughts when Standing Bird dropped the stone to signal the start. She managed to gather her muscles and spring forward to strike the water at the same moment as Long Walker.

Quickly she began to outdistance him, sliding through the water with smooth efficiency. She reached the ledge, grasped one of the sticks, and turned. She thrust the twig between her teeth and pushed away from the rock shelf.

Eagle Woman had hardly started her next stroke before she collided forcibly with the rapidly approaching Long Walker. Half stunned, she floundered for a moment, then surfaced, disoriented. At arm's length Walker was just picking up his willow twig from the rock ledge.

The girl resumed her swim for a moment before she realized that her mouth was empty. The willow cutting was gone. She must have lost it when she collided with Walker and choked. Frantically she stopped, treading water while she searched for the stick.

By the time she located the object, floating gently with the current, Long Walker had completed his turn and was churning toward the other shore. Eagle Woman quickly retrieved her stick and resumed the race, but she knew she had lost. All the way to the starting point the girl swam with the splashing thrust of her opponent's feet kicking water to foam ahead of her.

She could think only one thought—that she had lost this contest, the one of her own choice. Now the contestants were even again. It was distressing to realize that the past two days of exhausting, frustrating conflict had led exactly nowhere. The situation was exactly as it had been when she first attempted to join the Elk-dog Society.

Even worse, she realized, as she dragged herself from the water, it was now Walker's choice for the next contest. Unless, of course, he chose to discontinue the Challenge. But he would not do that, of course. He had now won the last two contests.

People were crowding around the winner, shouting congratulations and collecting bets from disgruntled losers. Eagle Woman staggered up the bank and stood, dripping water in puddles around her bare feet.

Standing Bird was beckoning to the two principals. They stumbled forward, facing each other in tired frustration. They were battered, sore, almost staggering. Their eyes met. Walker's left eye was partially swollen shut, corresponding to the dull ache in Eagle Woman's elbow. The collision in the water had been a forceful thing. The girl's lip was bruised, apparently from the force which had torn the willow twig from her teeth. She tasted the slight salty flavor of blood in her mouth.

More important to her was the stubborn expression on Long Walker's face. It said once again that he would never give up in his effort to prevent her attaining warrior status. Why must he be so?

The Elk-dog chieftain was speaking now, and Eagle Woman attempted to gather her wandering thoughts.

"—and I will not allow you to continue until you kill each other!"

He paused to frown at a ripple of laughter from the

crowd, then continued, as quiet resumed. "There will be only one more contest, and I will choose that. Then, whoever wins, it is over. Do you both understand this?"

The two young people nodded, too exhausted to question.

"Go, now," Standing Bird continued. "Tonight you must rest. The contest will be tomorrow."

He turned away, then paused for a moment as one of the onlookers called a question. The warrior turned with dignity and smiled a thin smile.

"What will the contest be?" he repeated. "A race! On foot, at a distance I shall choose."

Once again he turned and strode purposefully toward his lodge. Behind him the two young people stared dully at each other, neither ready to speak.

Around them excited talk was erupting, arguments beginning, wagers being placed. Eagle Woman and Long Walker turned wordlessly and shuffled toward their respective dwellings.

Bobcat fell into step beside his sister, chortling delightedly.

"*Aiee*, Eagle Woman, this is good! Running has always been one of your best efforts. You can defeat Long Walker!"

Numbly, the girl nodded halfhearted agreement.

13

>> >> >>

Standing Bird stood before the two contestants and the excited gathering of the People to mark the course for the race. Practically everyone in the Elk-dog band was assembled for the event. Wagering was good-natured and heavy.

Many of the members of the band thought the entire Challenge quite amusing, so there was much laughter and merriment. Also there was the excitement of this, the deciding race.

"Now, you understand," Standing Bird was saying to the two before him, "this is the final contest. There will be no more Challenge!"

Both nodded. The two young people had avoided contact, not even looking at each other this morning. Several among the band had noticed that both seemed only too anxious to finish the contest, to have it done. There were many who felt similarly, especially those who had no great love for wagering. It was all quite well to have a pleasant, amusing diversion such as this, but it was occupying the entire time and energies of the band. It was time to move on to other things.

Eagle Woman had startled many by appearing this morning in a dress. There was a murmur of apprehension on the part of her supporters, who felt that she might be ready to concede the race. Or was this a means to try to shame Long Walker? There was much quiet discussion as to her reasons.

Actually there was no deep mystery, no symbolism. It was a matter of practicality. Eagle Woman had worn men's garments for the past two days. The unfamiliar feel of the breechclout and leggings had begun to chafe her inner thighs and her groin. In planning for a running race, probably a long one, she felt she must dress as comfortably as possible. If she continued to wear the leggings, her skin would surely be rubbed raw and bleeding by the race's end.

In addition, Eagle Woman felt that she could run better in a skirt. She could lift it high to allow her long legs room to stretch, to lengthen her stride, and to cover more ground. She had done so many times during her childhood years. This would free her of the hampering constriction of leggings around thighs and hips.

As a precaution against the skirt itself becoming a problem, she had chosen her shortest dress. It was an old garment, well worn, one which allowed the fringe to fall above the knee. Then, as an extra precaution, she had taken a knife and slit the skirt up each side. There would be no danger of the garment restricting her stride.

Eagle Woman had spent some time with her uncle, the medicine man, on the previous evening. Owl had always given good advice and comfort to the girl as she grew up. On this occasion he had little to offer. She had asked his advice regarding whether she should continue the contest. Owl knew that no other person had any clue that her resolve was weakening. ▬

"You must do as you choose, Daughter. Only this—if you continue, you must do your best. It is no loss of pride to lose, unless you have done less than your finest try."

Eagle Woman had slipped back to her father's lodge, to rest and to try to prepare for the race. She had not actually considered abandoning her goal. It was only that in her exhaustion at the end of the gruelling second day she had begun to doubt herself a little. A bit of reassurance from Owl had been all that was needed. She was now ready.

Standing Bird raised his hand for silence, and the confusion quieted. Solemnly he pointed to a flat-topped hill on the horizon.

"You will run to that hill and return," he stated. "There are warriors there already. They have placed markers on a flat stone there. You will pick up one of the markers and return it here."

The forms of a handful of mounted warriors could now be seen against the sky on the hilltop, barely distinguishable in the distance.

Quickly Eagle Woman evaluated the situation. The most obvious route lay straight ahead, following the gully which meandered toward the hill. There would be one small stream to cross, some timber in the canyon, and perhaps a steep rocky shelf to climb, halfway there. It was not a truly difficult run.

To her right, however, slightly to the west of the valley, the land opened upon a high, flat plain. It would be level and fairly smooth, reaching along the canyon's rim almost to the foot of the hill that was the goal. This route would require, at first, that she climb a rather steep ridge to arrive at the level plain. She must also circle in a long arc to the west, following the canyon's curving rim. That would make a longer distance but might save time by avoiding the rougher going in the ravine.

Her decision was made by the time Standing Bird dropped the stone and called the signal to go. Long Walker, as she had expected, sprinted down the slope to follow the floor of the canyon. Eagle Woman turned to the right and began to jog toward the upland.

The first hundred paces were easy; then the broken rock of the hillside confronted her. She had been to this ridge many times. It was a quiet place to be alone, to think. She knew of a game trail, skirting along the rim as it ascended, and it was to this path that she slanted her course.

Even so, by the time she reached the top she was panting heavily. She caught a glimpse of Long Walker, running among the trees along the creek far below. He was well ahead of her, and she tried to reassure herself that she had accomplished a major part of the climb that Walker had yet before him.

Eagle Woman sprinted along the game trail which skirted the canyon's rim. How fortunate, the girl thought momentarily, that the trail was here. If she had had to study the terrain and plan the easiest route, much time would have been lost. As things were in the world, the trail had been there for many generations. Passing bands of deer, antelope, and elk had instinctively sought out the easiest course, and the hoofprints of their generations had permanently marked the path.

The trail wavered only slightly, dividing in places and being joined by other paths, but basically it skirted the rimrock. The going was good, and the girl could tell that she was gaining on Long Walker far below.

There was one place that brought some delay. A shallow spur canyon lay in her path. Trusting the instincts of long-departed deer, she followed the path straight toward the obstacle. The trail dipped among jumbled boulders, and she slowed to jump from rock to rock. She saw the reason for this slight deviation of the trail. There was a clear, sparkling spring among the rocks.

She would have welcomed a sip of the cool water but did not pause. She only moistened her drying lips with her tongue as she bounded up the other side of the gully and into the open again. Below her Long Walker was still in the lead, but he was now approaching an area of rough, broken rock and a forbidding outcrop which would slow him considerably. She smiled inwardly, trying to ignore the fact that her legs were beginning to ache.

Knifelike pains stabbed at her muscles with every motion. The girl knew this would pass and that she must keep running. Her breath came in ragged gasps. She felt that she had been running forever, unable to stop, though she knew the entire race would be less than half a sun's journey. That thought spurred her on, as she tried to ignore the pain in her chest and legs and the roaring in her ears.

Now she adjusted her course slightly to the left, swinging the arc toward the flat-topped hill. It was looming closer, and she could see the individual figures of mounted warriors on the hilltop.

She threw a quick glance to her left, where Long Walker now laboriously clambered over broken rim-rock to ascend the slope. Their paths would meet some distance ahead to begin the last ascent together. But, with a thrill, Eagle Woman realized that she was now ahead. Her strategy had been correct. She would start the last assault on the hill before Walker. Even more important was that he would be exhausted from fighting his way across the broken rock when he began the last slope.

Her heart leaped in triumph, and she filled her lungs with the fresh air of the prairie. Almost, now, the pain in her muscles had become bearable. She looked ahead, slowing to pace herself for the last steep climb. The warriors at the top were yelling and cheering, motioning her onward.

The last few steps to the flat summit seemed to take all the strength her tired legs could muster. The warriors pointed to a large flat stone, and the tired girl stumbled in that direction.

"There is your marker, Eagle Woman. Hurry!"

The speaker was her kinsman, Long Elk. Eagle Woman grasped one of the objects displayed on the flat rock. It was a small, smooth stone, polished by many summers of rolling in the stream. It was of a size to hold in one's palm, and it was comforting to squeeze it there as she turned to start the second half of the race.

With some amusement she noticed that there was a short strip of buckskin tied tightly around the stone and that it had been decorated with red and yellow paint. Standing Bird was taking no chances. None could accuse anyone of deceit, and none could question whether this was the proper stone or whether one had been substituted.

She was starting down the hill when she met Long Walker. He was breathing heavily, and his face was ashen. He did not look up as they passed but continued to labor forward.

Eagle Woman felt sorry. She longed to stop, to sit down together and talk, but she was not deceived. Walker would never give up. He would gain on her on the descent and might even be able to catch up.

But she thought not. From the time that she met and passed the exhausted Walker, Eagle Woman began to allow herself to admit a little confidence. By the time she approached the rocky cleft with the spring, she risked a look backward.

Long Walker had indeed gained somewhat, but she saw no way, short of accident, that he could catch her now. She even paused a moment to take a handful of water from the clear pool before she bounded ahead.

The horsemen were overtaking her now, shouting and waving as they rode alongside. Through the aching in her chest, the burning lungs, and the sharp pains in her muscles, she began to feel the triumph of victory.

She had won.

14

>> >> >>

Long Walker was only too aware that he was beaten. He realized that he had chosen the wrong route when he saw Eagle Woman on the slope ahead of him. When she passed him on her way back down, Walker despaired, but he still hoped to catch her.

If only, he had thought for a moment, they could sit and talk. Perhaps he could make her understand that all his efforts were for her own good. The pursuits that the girl was proposing to enter were too dangerous. He wanted to shelter and protect her.

Walker would have been astonished if he had known how close to his own fantasies were those of the girl. He imagined the two of them in their own lodge, Eagle Woman sometimes with him on a hunt, but above all, together. They had never yet finished talking. There were always things to discuss, to enjoy, to share together.

But in the past few suns he had seen this possibility slipping away. Long Walker could imagine in his mind's eye the two of them together, even if the girl attained warrior status. Only he was certain that Eagle Woman would not accept it.

So, he had reasoned, he must stop her, and the Challenge had been his last resort. He had not been happy at its progress. Eagle Woman's skills were even greater than he realized. Walker resented the attitude of the onlookers, the wagers, the ribald jokes. And now it had come to the last contest, and it would be over.

He knew he was beaten by the time Eagle Woman stopped for a sip of water at the spring. He had elected to follow her course and had in fact gained considerably on her by the time they approached the camp. Horsemen rode alongside both runners, people yelled, dogs barked. Walker had managed to draw nearer, near enough for a respectable contest, but he knew that it was not good enough. There would be a certain amount of good-natured ridicule. That was not his primary concern. The depressing thought which weighed him down as he labored toward the finish was that he had failed in his effort to protect and shelter his friend, Eagle Woman. Worse still, she would always hate him for the attempt.

The girl ahead of him sprinted across the finish line, skirt flying and long legs flashing. Walker put forth his best effort and pounded across to hand his marker to Standing Bird. A circle of people gathered around the exhausted contestants as the Elk-dog leader spoke.

"Eagle Woman, you have met the Challenge. You are now ready to be one of us in the Elk-dog Society."

The girl nodded, panting heavily, trying to catch her breath. Long Walker struggled toward her, his color pale, sick from his effort but even more from his failure.

"You have done well, Eagle Woman," he gasped.

She looked up and smiled at him. It was a triumphant smile, but friendly—a trifle surprised, perhaps. Long Walker permitted himself a glimmer of optimism. Was there, somewhere beneath the girl's confi-

dent exterior, still a warm spot for him in her heart?
The possibility was there, and he would pursue it.

But later. Just now it seemed to require all his attention merely to breathe in and out. He sank to a sitting
position, heart still pounding and lungs gasping for
air. His muscles ached. He wondered for a moment if
Eagle Woman could possibly feel this much pain and
exhaustion. He looked over at the girl being warmly
congratulated by friends and family. The pain of
winning, he reflected morosely, is certainly less than
that of losing.

He was breathing more slowly now and managed to
struggle to his feet. What would the girl do now, he
wondered. Would she seek a vision quest and insist on
going on a war party? His old concerns came flooding
back into his mind.

He could protect her, to a degree, in a war party; he
could make her safety his primary concern. There was
no way, however, that he could help her in the soli-
tary aloneness of the vision quest. It was forbidden for
any to follow her.

Perhaps, he thought, she would stop here. She had
won warrior status and might be willing to rest at that
point. Even as these thoughts occurred to him, he
knew better.

Eagle Woman was sipping cautiously from a water
skin held by her brother, Bobcat. Someone thrust a
similar vessel at Long Walker, and he gratefully rinsed
his parched mouth, spat on the ground, and sipped
again.

Standing Bird was motioning again to Eagle Woman
and Long Walker. The two approached the chief, sur-
rounded by excited onlookers and more serious members of the Elk-dog Society.

"Now, Eagle Woman, how will you be called?"

"I do not understand, my chief."

"What do you wish as your name? You may wait
until after your vision quest if you wish."

Long Walker had not proceeded this far in his thinking. He had forgotten that it would be the girl's right

as a warrior to change her name to one of her choosing. She might choose to do so now or after her vision quest, or even at a later time to commemorate some important event. Walker was certain that she would choose to honor the events of this day.

He was correct. Eagle Woman considered only briefly, then spoke to Standing Bird.

"Yes, my chief. I will choose now." She paused a moment, looking long at the flat-topped hill in the distance and all it had symbolized. "I will honor the race, the contest which has made me a warrior. I will be called Running Eagle!"

Standing Bird nodded. "It is good!"

He looked around the circle. "Know you all," he proclaimed solemnly, "that she who has been called Eagle Woman will now be called *Running* Eagle Woman."

"No!" The girl almost shouted at him. "Not 'woman.' I will be called *Running Eagle*."

15
>> >> >>

The vision quest of Running Eagle was undertaken immediately. Her parents, her brother Bobcat, and her friend Long Walker all spent much time in worry and concern. The danger of her remaining alone in a remote place while she fasted and dreamed was considerable, of course.

Sweet Grass fretted, and Eagle tried to pretend lack of concern to reassure his wife. Long Walker suffered in solitude, unable to share his worries with anyone. Bobcat came as close as any to a real understanding of the situation.

"She is all right," he assured his mother. "Has she not proved herself as a warrior?"

Bobcat was enough older than his sister to have assumed a protective, almost proprietary air as they grew up. He had encouraged her in her boyish endeavors and had taken great pride in her achievements. It was he who had nominated her as a warrior sister.

When the girl had requested warrior status, Bobcat

was proud, yet mildly amused. Only during the increasing tension of the Challenge and its contests had he begun to feel strongly about it. By the time his sister had successfully proved herself, he was her most enthusiastic supporter.

Even so, Bobcat understood her. He saw behind the busy, almost frantic activity to the sensitive emotions of the girl who had always looked up to him as an older brother, to be admired and honored. He was not deceived by her apparent anger, almost hatred, toward Long Walker. Bobcat had recognized the closeness between the two contestants in the Challenge and rejoiced in it.

Long Walker was one of few young men he had ever known that Bobcat considered worthy of his sister. Walker was an acceptable brother-in-law, one the entire family could receive with pride.

Bobcat knew his sister well. He was certain that once she had proved her point, Eagle Woman, now Running Eagle, would be ready to settle back and let her budding friendship blossom into marriage. Many young women rode with their husbands in the hunt, and this was the sort of mannish thing that would appeal to Running Eagle.

He smiled to himself in amusement at the thought. He was perhaps the only one who knew how deeply rooted were her womanly instincts after all. Bobcat alone was aware of the contents of the hidden package behind the lodge lining. The girl had long ago confided to her brother that she was gathering cooking stones for her future as head of her own lodge.

So Bobcat was unconcerned, in the long run, as to the ultimate outcome of all this. With tolerant amusement he knew that, when she was ready, his headstrong sister would reveal her plans. Until then it was no one's concern but hers. Even though Bobcat knew that young Walker need have no worry about the eventual outcome, he could do nothing to reassure him. To do so would betray the confidence of Eagle Woman.

Running Eagle, that is. *Aiee*, he would have a difficult time until the new name became comfortable.

The camp had been quiet since the end of the Challenge. It had been only a few suns when Running Eagle announced that she would go on her vision quest. It was her right to do so, but still her family was uneasy.

Bobcat knew that the girl's friend Walker would also be concerned, so he made occasion to spend time with him after Running Eagle had departed. True to their respect for her, neither mentioned the thoughts that concerned them both—the safety of Running Eagle. They discussed the weather, the hunt, tribal politics, and where they were likely to camp for the winter, but the girl was never mentioned. It was as if she did not exist.

Running Eagle had taken no food, only weapons and a water skin to sustain her through the days of her fast. She chose for her protection her bow, her short knife, and a light war club. It was a weapon that had never appealed to her, but her brother had urged her to take it. It could do no harm.

Bobcat had watched the girl set out, on foot and alone, with an odd premonition of danger. Strangely, though he felt that she was quite capable of taking care of herself, there was a sadness, a permanence, about this parting.

He continued to be uneasy as the days passed, feeling moody and depressed. He could not have explained it, this vague sensation of loss and separation. He told himself that it was only because he now faced the loss of his sister, who would come of age through the ritual of the vision quest.

He felt a great deal of relief, however, when a diversion offered itself. Bobcat had been for a cooling swim in the long, hot afternoon and was just stepping from the water when two of his friends rode up.

"*Ah-koh*, Bobcat," called Dark Cloud. "Get your horse and come with us."

"Where?"

"There are antelope near Cedar Creek," he pointed to the south. "Some of us are going on a hunt!"

Bobcat was already pulling on his leggings. *Aiee*, this was what he needed.

16
>> >> >>

Running Eagle stood at the edge of a rocky hilltop, looking once more at the world that had been hers for the past four suns. She hated to leave; the vision quest had been so satisfying and fulfilling.

She did not know what she had expected, but there was no way to describe the experience. The first pangs of hunger had given up and ceased to gnaw on the second day. It was after that that the brightness, the color, and the clarity of the world became apparent. It was true both in wakefulness and in her dream visions. She wandered in her mind's eye across the rolling prairie, not distinguishing dream from reality. She found herself inside the thoughts of the creatures around her. The timid maternal concern of the quail on her eggs under an overhanging grass clump was plain to her. Just as plain was the confidence of a majestic, old bull elk, his new antlers still furry at this season. She communed with an otter, who laughed at her over the accident in the swimming challenge. The thoughts of a rabbit who nibbled grass near the stone where she sat complimented her on her race, and she smiled.

In her delight at the ability to commune with all these creatures, she almost forgot that her mission was partly to search for her medicine animal. It was really no great surprise to her, however. Somehow, she had known it would be an eagle.

The puzzling thing was that nothing much transpired. She found it more difficult to understand the eagle than any of the other creatures. It merely came, sat on a broken dead tree stub at the rim of the canyon, and looked at her.

In vain, Running Eagle searched for some message, some meaning. The proud gaze of the bird was inspiring, uplifting, and seemed somehow urgent. But there was no apparent purpose, no direction. Ah well, perhaps it would come later. She remembered that her father had once said it was years before he understood his medicine animal.

She awoke and found that it had indeed been a sleep-dream. The sun was rising, and the prairie was coming alive for a new day. In the low spots along the stream, scraps of fog hung like wisps of smoke among the trees. The world was good.

Running Eagle took a little water from the skin and raised the chanting melody of the Morning Song to Sun Boy in the east. So great was her pleasure, her exaggerated enjoyment with the experience, that she felt she could stay here indefinitely. She knew otherwise, of course, but it was a delightful fantasy. She really must begin her return journey today to the camp of the People.

There were advantages to that, she realized. It would be good to break her fast, to eat again, though she felt no urgency in it. It would also be good to be with her family again, to feel its affection and support. She could talk with her brother and share some of her feelings about the vision quest. Some, but not all.

Best of all, she now admitted to herself as she gathered her few belongings, she would soon see Walker.

She was ready to forget her petty anger at him. She did not fully understand his reasons for the Challenge, but was willing to forgive him. Now, her vision quest behind her, she could begin to think again in terms of sharing his lodge.

She hung the club at her waist, picked up her bow and arrows, and swung her robe across her shoulder. She took a last glance around her camp site and then another long look at the green expanse of prairie, as if she had never seen it so clearly before. She turned toward the game trail which picked its way down the steep side of the hill.

Sun Boy was high before Running Eagle stopped by a shady spring of sparkling water. She drank long and deep, rested for a time, and moved on.

Shadows were lengthening before she saw the faint blue haze of smoke from the lodge fires of the People. She hurried on. Soon the conical shapes of the scattered lodges could be seen in the gathering dusk.

Then she noticed a strange sound, a prolonged wail, rising and falling in pitch but continuous in intensity. Alarmed, she stopped to listen. In a moment she was able to identify the cadence of the Mourning Song. Something was terribly wrong.

Anxiously she sprang forward, yet she forced herself to pace her stride and conserve her strength in order to reach the camp. Questions pounded in her head: Who was dead? What had happened? What was wrong?

Breathing hard, she trotted among the first of the lodges, looking for someone to ask. An old woman hobbled along, wailing loudly. Running Eagle caught at her arm, but the woman pulled away and staggered on, paying no attention.

The girl hurried toward a cluster of people near the center of the village, searching for someone to ask. The first person she encountered was Long Walker.

"Walker!" she shouted above the piercing wail of the Mourning Song. "What is it? What has happened?"

"Eagle Woman!"

Long Walker took both her hands in his, tragedy

stark on his face. She ignored his unconscious use of her former name.

"Head Splitters stole part of the horse herd," he began.

"Yes?"

"Some of our young men tried to stop them. Three were killed."

"Three Head Splitters?"

"No, three of the People. No Head Splitters. Eagle Woman—"

He paused, and the import of this news finally sank home. The girl grasped at his arm.

"Walker!" she demanded. "Who?"

"Your brother, Bobcat."

17
>> >> >>

The story was simple, so pitifully simple, as Walker related it to her. They were walking as rapidly as was practical toward the lodge of her parents.

It had been one of the not uncommon horse-stealing raids of the Head Splitters. Not more than ten of the enemy were involved. They had carefully crept upon an isolated portion of the herd, frightened the two youths who were guarding it, and quickly drove away some thirty animals at a wild gallop.

The problem had developed when the enemy and the stolen horses neared Cedar Creek. They had apparently blundered into the area where Bobcat and his friends were hunting antelope, and there was an encounter between the two groups of surprised young men.

The People were outnumbered more than two to one, and there was not much of a battle. Dark Cloud had seen one Head Splitter fall and another appear to be wounded. Of the young hunters of the People, he alone had escaped.

The search party had just returned, bringing the bodies of the fallen warriors. Mourning was in full cry, and a council fire had already been prepared.

Running Eagle lifted the lodge-door skin and slipped inside, thanking Walker briefly for his concern. Her mother was crouched near the fire, wailing the somber cadences of the Mourning Song. The face of Sweet Grass was streaked with dirt, ashes, and tears in the ritual of mourning the crossing over of loved ones.

Eagle sat nearby, ready to give comfort. His crippled leg extended straight before him, and his face, also, was stained with tears. Running Eagle gave each of them a quick embrace and turned to the dark, robe-enveloped form beside the doorway. Her tears were flowing freely.

Even at this tense moment, the girl allowed herself to wonder. Would she be expected to carry on the grief ritual as a woman would?

The answer came swiftly. No. Bobcat had believed strongly in her right to aspire to warrior status. She would live up to his expectations. She could cry, as any warrior might, but she must avenge this death. She dropped to her knees and gently touched the furry robe that enclosed this world's remains of her brother. His spirit, she knew, had probably already crossed over.

"My brother," she said softly, "I will bring vengeance!"

There was a call outside. The criers of the warrior societies were walking through the camp, announcing that the council fire was lighted. Running Eagle and her father rose and hastened toward the fire.

Heads Off, as band chief, convened the council and omitted the ritual smoke to the four winds. He glanced around the circle of chiefs, and the council began.

"My brothers, you know why we are here. It falls to our brother Standing Bird to lead a war party. His are the fallen warriors."

The Elk-dog Society's leader rose, and his speech

was quick and to the point. "We will leave tonight and travel by moon's light. Who will go?"

A dozen young warriors sprang to their feet, Running Eagle among them. Long Walker, also standing, started to protest but then remained silent. There was no way he could deny her the right to be a part of the war party. A member of her family had been killed.

"We will meet there," Standing Bird pointed to the meadow, "when the moon rises."

Running Eagle walked with her father back toward the lodge. She must find her horse, ready her weapons, and prepare to depart. Sweet Grass would have food ready for her to carry.

"The horses are over there," her father pointed. "The herders brought them in after the raid."

Eagle accompanied his daughter to the area where the young men held the milling animals.

"Running Eagle!" a young man called respectfully. "Your gray mare is there!"

The girl shook out her rope and moved among the animals. She crooned quietly as she moved alongside the gray and slipped the rope smoothly around the mare's slim throat. Quickly she looped the medicine-knot around the lower jaw and threw a leg over the mare's back to swing up.

Eagle limped beside the mare's shoulder. "You will be careful, my daughter?"

"Of course, Father!"

They reached the lodge, and Sweet Grass handed a small packet of dried food to the girl. Running Eagle paused only long enough to embrace her parents and pick up her weapons, then remounted.

The red-orange rim of the rising moon was beginning to show as the girl trotted into the meadow to meet the others. Only a day past full, it would provide enough light to travel swiftly. It should be easy to track a large number of horses across open ground, even by moonlight.

Running Eagle could follow the thoughts of Standing Bird, leader of the war party. The retreating Head

Splitters would stop for the night to rest, graze, and water their captured horses. By traveling all night, the pursuers could probably overtake them not long after daylight.

Standing Bird took a long look at his warriors and called softly. "Dark Cloud?"

"Yes, my chief?"

"Take us to the place where you last saw the Head Splitters."

Of course the People knew the way, thought Running Eagle. They had retrieved their dead from that area. The chief only wished to honor Dark Cloud, the sole survivor of the skirmish, and provide him some of the prestige he might have lost in defeat. Yes, Standing Bird was a wise leader.

The party traveled rapidly, but it carefully spared its horses by frequent changes of pace and occasional rest stops. It would do no good to overtake the enemy, only to be handicapped by exhausted horses.

During one of the stops Running Eagle sat watching the slow march of the Seven Hunters around the Real-star. How close they looked tonight. It was a night that could have been beautiful except for the tragic nature of their mission. A night bird called from a ravine to their left, and the soft, silent form of a great hunting owl blotted out a handful of stars for a moment as it passed.

Someone strolled up beside her and stood for a moment, hesitating. She glanced up to see the stern profile of Long Walker against the moonlit sky in the east.

"Running Eagle," he began hesitantly.

"Yes, Walker?"

"I would be honored if you would fight by my side tomorrow."

The girl paused for a moment before answering. She was puzzled and perhaps a trifle suspicious. Was this an acknowledgment of her warrior status? Or was he suggesting that she needed his protection?

She burned inwardly with the thought but said nothing. It was possible that the young man was merely trying to be friendly. She could meet him halfway.

"Who knows," she observed casually, "where we may be when the battle starts?"

"May I ride with you?"

"You may ride wherever you wish."

Long Walker heaved a long sigh. Ah well, it was better than nothing. He squatted beside her for a moment.

But now warriors were swinging to their horses. Standing Bird was signaling that it was time to depart.

18
» » »

Standing Bird noticed immediately that the girl and Long Walker rode together after the stop. It was his place as a leader to note such things.

He was pleased. It had been a matter of some concern to him that two young people whom he had always liked had come to the bitterness that had been evident in the Challenge.

Now he wondered exactly what had occurred at the rest stop. Was it Walker's concern for the girl's safety that made him ride by her side? It was certain that if that was the purpose, Walker had concealed it from Running Eagle. The girl would angrily refuse his assistance.

It must be, then, that Long Walker had found some diplomatic way to achieve the right to ride with her. Standing Bird smiled, amused. Walker was an able young man whose thoughts were good. He would be a chief some day. Perhaps even a great leader. He had participated in two war parties and had shown bravery. More important, he had shown good judgment.

Yes, it was good that Long Walker rode beside the

young warrior woman. He could be depended upon to guide her on her first war party.

Standing Bird well remembered his own first war party. He had been led into battle by Heads Off, the girl's grandfather. It had been the first use of Elk-dogs by the People. Their victory over the Head Splitters that day was immortalized in song, story, and dance as the Great Battle.

Aiee, how time had flown. The two sons of Heads Off were now grown and with families of their own. One had become a respected medicine man, the other, Eagle, would have undoubtedly been a great chief if it had not been for his crippled leg. Still, he was honored and respected for his knowledge. And never were there two finer children than Bobcat and Eagle Woman. No, Running Eagle.

How Eagle must have longed to ride on this war party, to assist his daughter and to avenge his son. Standing Bird's heart went out to his friend. He could understand the loss. When no more than a child, he had lost his own father in a Head Splitter raid.

He was uneasy about the girl. If something happened to her, the family of Eagle would be effectively finished. Ah well, such were the worries of a leader. Running Eagle could take care of herself. He smiled to himself in amusement at the thought. *Aiee*, some Head Splitter would be in for a surprise!

Just before dawn, with the party proceeding cautiously, the advance scouts returned to report that the night camp of the Head Splitters was ahead. Standing Bird knew the ritual well. They would approach the enemy, who could scarcely escape unless they abandoned the horses. In that case they would recover the stolen herd and perhaps count honors on a couple of the fleeing Head Splitters. That would even the score, and the escaping warriors would carry the message that the People had exacted vengeance.

Another possibility was that the enemy would wish to parley. Standing Bird had seen it before. In an extreme confrontation they might claim that they had not stolen these Elk-dogs, merely found them, and any killing must have been done by others. Then, depending on the mood of the two parties, they might recover the horses without a fight.

Unless, of course, someone started the hostilities. It would be touchy and unpredictable, with much circling, conversing in the sign talk, and bragging on both sides before it could be determined just how it would go.

All this, of course, was why it was well to have Long Walker close by the side of the girl, to explain the progression of events.

The Head Splitters had started to move with the coming of Sun Boy. They must have suspected some pursuit.

The pursuers passed the night camp quickly and pushed ahead. The trail was fresh, and it became apparent that the encounter would take place in a large, open valley ahead.

They topped the last hill and saw the retreating horse herd. Almost at the same instant the enemy appeared to become aware of the war party. There was much pointing, and warriors rode around the horse herd, bunching them together.

So, thought Standing Bird, they will make a stand. Cautiously he led his war party forward. To his left was Long Walker, and beyond him, the girl. The rest of the warriors spread out in a solid front to each side as they advanced. The Head Splitters did likewise.

It now became apparent that the strength of the enemy had been underestimated. Perhaps Dark Cloud had not seen all of the raiders. Perhaps they had been joined by more. It did not matter now how it had happened. The important thing was that Standing Bird's party of fifteen now appeared outnumbered by three or four, counting horse herders. If there were to be a parley at all, the enemy raiders would be able to negotiate from a position of strength.

It was with some indecision and dread that Standing Bird now led his party forward.

The enemy leader appeared to be a large, heavyset man who sat calmly in the center of the line, watching the People approach. The rest of the party, Standing Bird noted, were younger men. A party much like his own, then. Two or three experienced warriors, the rest just starting to earn honors.

Some of the raiders appeared fidgety, and one young man's horse, near the center of the line, kept prancing nervously. It collided with the horse of the man next to him. That horse, in turn, swung broadside to the advancing party.

The People were not quite close enough to begin the sign talk yet, but they were close enough to recognize the turned horse. There was no other like it. The color was a dark mouse-gray, and on the left hip was a scatter of white patches of irregular shape and size. Bobcat had been teased about leaving his horse tied beneath an owl's nest, but it had never bothered him. He had affectionately called the rawboned gelding Owl Dung.

Standing Bird turned to see if the girl recognized her brother's mount, but he was a moment too late. He was only in time to see Running Eagle jab heels into the flanks of her startled mare and charge, alone, straight at the enemy.

His other warriors sat dumbfounded, in the process of readying their weapons.

"*Aiee!*" someone said softly.

Long Walker was the first to react. The girl's gray mare had covered only three jumps before Walker's big bay leaped forward under his urgent heel. As he charged he raised his head to give vent to the battle cry. The deep-throated, chilling sound of the People's war cry resounded across the prairie.

Perhaps it was this sound that pushed the others into action. An echo of the yell burst from a dozen throats as Standing Bird led his warriors in a thundering frontal charge, trying in vain to overtake the girl on the catlike gray mare.

19
>> >> >>

Black Fox had been uneasy since the beginning of the raiding party. Things had gone too well. He and Sitting Bear, slightly older than he, had organized the raid.

They would take a handful of aspiring young Head Splitters into the country of the Elk-dog People to gain experience. There would be an opportunity to steal a few good horses, perhaps kidnap a young woman or two. There might even be a skirmish, a chance for the best and boldest of the novices to count their first honors in battle.

And things had gone well under the experienced guidance of Sitting Bear. The war party had located the summer camp of the enemy without difficulty. It had been almost too simple to carry out the raid on the horse herd. It had been a thing of great amusement to see the terror-struck youths who guarded the herd scramble in panic before the raiders. It had been almost too easy.

Then they had encountered the small hunting party.

These had been more experienced young warriors. They had fought bravely. The Head Splitters had sustained wounds but had defeated the outnumbered hunters very quickly. One survivor had been allowed to escape to carry the tale of Head Splitter victory.

The raiding party had continued homeward, driving the stolen herd, now expanded with the mounts of the slain hunters. It had been at this point that Black Fox began to be more seriously concerned.

He could not exactly define his anxiety. It was a subtle thing, an undefined feeling. Everything had gone so smoothly, so easily. The young warriors joked and laughed as they rode, now confident and boastful after their brief baptism of battle. Perhaps that was what concerned Black Fox. The youths were too confident.

He glanced across to the leader of the party, to see if he felt the uneasiness, too. Sitting Bear was relaxed, smiling, chatting amiably with a couple of admiring young warriors as they rode.

No, thought Black Fox. Sitting Bear does not feel it. But what is it?

He tried to define his uneasiness, reviewing the events of the past two suns. They would undoubtedly be pursued by the Elk-dog People. Perhaps that was a matter for concern.

But no, that was not likely. The pursuing party would be small. They would not risk leaving the village undefended. At most the pursuit would consist of no more than their own party's strength.

There would be a confrontation of sorts. The pursuers would claim the horses; there would be much arguing and many boasts and threats. Then, depending on the relative strength of the two opposing parties, some horses might be given up or a refusal accepted. It was unlikely that a pitched battle would ensue.

Except for one thing, Black Fox reminded himself. Possibly it was this thought that had continued to worry him. It had to do with the identity of the band whose horse herd they had raided. He was of the opinion that this was the Southern band of the Elk-

dog People. That group had been a thorn in the flesh
of the Head Splitters for a generation, since their hair-
faced outsider had brought the first Elk-dogs.

The hair-faced chief was old now, of course, and no
longer active in battle. Still, his was the most able of
bands, daring and resourceful. Their unorthodox conduct in battle had resulted in the defeat of the Head
Splitters, even under the able chiefs Gray Wolf, Lean
Bull, and Bull's Tail. The last, though he had lived
through his defeat, was convinced that some powerful,
some supernatural medicine guarded this band. Bull's
Tail had never been quite the same since the disaster
at the cliff now called Medicine Rock.

Black Fox mentioned his doubts to Sitting Bear,
who scoffed at the whole idea.

"Look, Fox. We have stolen their best horses, killed
three of their strongest young warriors. Why do you
worry?"

Still Black Fox worried. He cast backward glances,
looking for any sign of pursuit. It was no surprise,
then, when he spied the riders behind them. There
was actually a sense of relief. He could handle anything, he felt, better than the uncertainty he had experienced. He shifted his weapons to readiness and relaxed
to await the confrontation.

There was a flurry of excitement among the young
warriors, quieted with a gesture by Sitting Bear. Now
would come the posturing, threats, and discussion,
followed by the skirmish, if any. Black Fox slumped
comfortably until it was determined the extent of
participation that would be required. Through narrowed lids he evaluated the approaching warriors.

He quickly saw that his own group slightly outnumbered the newcomers. Good. They could probably
bluff through the argument without bloodshed.

The older warrior near the center was probably their
leader. Black Fox had seen the man before. What was
his name? Walking Bird? No, *Standing* Bird. Yes, this
was the man. A subchief of the Southern band, head
of one of the warrior societies, perhaps.

Black Fox had seen him as the two tribes encountered each other casually each season while on the move. These contacts were brief and almost cordial, though cautious. There was no conflict when both groups had women and children with them. It would be too dangerous to involve the families.

So Black Fox now identified Standing Bird as the leader. The other members of the party appeared to be younger warriors, efficient-looking, possibly with some degree of experience.

At precisely that moment Black Fox was startled to see a slim youth on a gray horse leap forward into a charge. The thing was so ridiculous that it took a moment to realize what was happening. In fact he thought at first that the young warrior's horse had merely bolted out of control. In the space of a few heartbeats, however, it became apparent that the charge was deliberate. The slim youth was hammering heels into the gray mare's flanks and beginning to sound the war cry of the Elk-dog People in a high-pitched falsetto.

It was wrong. This was no way to conduct a battle. It should be left to the leaders to argue, exchange insults, and, in the final decision, lead the fight or arrange the terms.

But this novice warrior apparently did not understand the ritual. He was launching a deliberate charge without waiting for the confrontation and arguments.

Black Fox glanced at the rest of his own party. Sitting Bear was staring open-mouthed, and the younger warriors sat or milled about nervously. Black Fox looked back at the charging young warrior and discovered that a tall, capable-looking warrior on a big bay stallion had joined the charge. Close behind thundered the entire party of pursuers, led by Standing Bird. Their full-throated war cry echoed across the meadow as the distance between the two groups closed.

Black Fox, sitting apart from the major thrust of the attack, saw the clash develop before his eyes. The slim youth in the lead was charging straight at Sitting Bear, who still sat dumbfounded.

Then Black Fox had a startling realization. The charging young warrior, swiftly bearing down on the raiders, was no warrior at all, but a *woman*. A crazy, completely mad woman, for some obscure reason riding with a war party.

Close behind her pounded the tall warrior on the bay stallion, readying his lance. Still, it was the woman who struck the first blow of the battle, an arrow thrown with unerring accuracy at the bare midriff of Sitting Bear. The chief, just readying his war club for the clash, slid limply from his horse instead.

Black Fox urged his horse forward but could not reach the center of the action before the two groups met. A young warrior swung his club at the crazy woman, but she avoided his blow by swinging nimbly to the side of her horse. The club whistled through empty air. A moment later the warrior who wielded it fell heavily before the lance charge of the tall man on the bay.

Now he and the woman were completely circled by young Head Splitters, fighting to free themselves. The woman loosed another arrow, and yet another, then cast her bow aside to swing a light war club. The man at her side used his lance until pressed too closely for working room. Then he, too, turned to the war club.

The two had made great inroads against the Head Splitters but were now becoming hard-pressed. Then the main force, led by Standing Bird, struck the fight. The new pressure was too much for the inexperienced horse raiders.

Black Fox, not yet even able to enter the conflict, pushed forward in frustration. Before his eyes his novice warriors began to panic. The rout became contagious, and in a moment the entire raiding party was in full flight, except for the handful lying dead or dying around Crazy Woman and her companion.

For a moment Black Fox considered a charge at the two, but he reconsidered. He had not survived to his present status by being foolhardy. He and his warriors, by this time in full flight, were now outnumbered. In addition, there was much he did not understand about this situation.

Why, for instance, had the Elk-dog warriors followed Crazy Woman in her unorthodox charge? True, he had now seen her at close range and had observed that this was one of the most beautiful women he had ever seen.

Yet among his own people that should have been all the more reason to keep her close to the lodge. Black Fox was sure that a night in his bed would break her spirit and make her forget such foolishness as going on war parties. Women of his tribe would never be allowed such activities.

And what of her tall companion, he of the bay stallion? What was his part in this?

Reluctantly Black Fox turned away. He must, to save his own skin. He cast one last look at the beautiful warrior woman and the tall man at her side.

He would remember those two.

20
›› ›› ››

When Running Eagle sprang forward in the spectacular charge that resulted in a rout, she had no such idea in mind. Rather it was because of her inexperience. In her naivete she assumed that when one sees and identifies the quarry that it is proper to attack.

So while others were preparing weapons, waiting for the chiefs to start a parley, she initiated her charge. She was enraged that a member of the raiding party boldly rode Owl Dung, her brother's horse. Her rage, however, did not affect her judgment. Many times she had heard her grandfather speak of tactics in battle.

"Strike the enemy's leader first," Heads Off counseled. "Then the others are without leadership."

With this thought in the back of her mind, Running Eagle charged straight at the burly warrior near the center of the line who appeared to be the enemy leader. The horse thief riding Owl Dung would be second. Not until she had loosed her first arrow and observed the man's sliding collapse did she realize that she was virtually alone. Only Long Walker had followed her closely. He was thrusting savagely with his lance, effectively striking the circling warriors around them.

Running Eagle was still puzzled. Where were Standing Bird and the other Elk-dog warriors? She had little time to wonder, as she loosed her second arrow at the man on her brother's horse.

It was not until after she had abandoned her bow in favor of the war club that Standing Bird's warriors struck. In a moment the Head Splitters were running in panic, leaving their dead and wounded behind.

There was one disquieting encounter. As the enemy retreated, one tall young chief seemed reluctant to leave. Running Eagle thought the man was about to charge and readied herself for the clash. Instead the other looked long and hard at her, then turned his horse abruptly to ride away. She had an odd premonition about this man, a feeling that they would meet again.

Now some Elk-dog warriors of Standing Bird were milling around, shouting the war cry. Some pursued the fleeing Head Splitters a short distance; others began to gather the excited horse herd. Long Walker reined in beside her. His presence was comforting, as the excitement of the conflict began to be replaced by the weak-kneed realization of what had happened.

"*Aiee!* Did you intend to fight them all, by yourself?"

Long Walker's face was still flushed with victory, his eyes flashing and his smile broad and companionable. Both knew that they had fought well together, and the feeling was good.

But now Running Eagle began to realize that she had made a mistake in her lone charge. It must be that there were rules, like those of the hunt, that the leader of the war party must say when to begin. *Aiee*, how stupid of her! She glanced around, embarrassed, to see the reaction of the other warriors. Most were riding back and forth in wild celebration. A few looted the weapons from enemy dead, some raced after loose horses.

Standing Bird rode up, seemed about to speak, then changed his mind. He nodded in recognition, expression unchanging. The girl was keenly aware that he might have severely criticized her. He had apparently chosen not to do so at this time. She wondered whether she would still be called before the warrior society for punishment. Perhaps she could speak to Walker about it.

Three young riders trotted past, singing triumphantly.

"—and she has killed the enemy, and stolen back the horses—"

Embarrassed, Running Eagle realized that she was the object of their song. Close on the heels of this thought came another. Her companions were regarding her lone charge as an act of bravery, not one of insubordination. This, in all probability, was the reason for Standing Bird's indecisiveness. She turned to him.

"My chief, I did not understand—"

Standing Bird shook his head gently. "It is nothing. It has turned out well. But, next time . . ."

Running Eagle nodded, ashamed. "Yes, my chief."

Standing Bird ended the matter with a wave of his hand and rode away. Nothing more was said.

A young man rode up, leading a riderless horse. He handed the rein to the girl.

"Your brother's horse, Running Eagle."

She nodded her thanks. Only now was coming the full impact of their mission's purpose, and her voice was choked into silence by this reminder of her loss.

The riders were surrounding the horse herd now, skillfully keeping the excited animals milling in a circle while they began to calm. When they appeared under control, the horsemen began to urge the herd back toward the village.

It had been a highly successful mission. They had punished the Head Splitters severely, killing several and counting many honors. The People had lost only one warrior, and two were slightly wounded. Because of the mounts of the dead raiders, they had recovered more horses than were originally stolen. This would be regarded as a great joke for many seasons, as long as the story was resung.

Except, brooded Running Eagle, it does not bring back Bobcat. How unfair that her brother should be struck down in his prime. It did not seem to be a part of the scheme of things. It would have been easier, perhaps, to give him up if the cause had been more sensible—an accident in the hunt, or even a loss in battle on a war party.

But a meaningless thing such as this she could not accept. Bobcat had done nothing except to be in the wrong place at the wrong time. She tried to console herself with the thought that her brother had died bravely. She was unsuccessful. Her thoughts kept coming back to two ideas. One, that the death of Bobcat was somehow not intended to be. It was a flaw, an error in the world's pattern.

The other thought was that the interruption, the flaw, had been caused by a deliberate action on the part of the Head Splitters. For this, for the death of her brother, the enemy must be punished.

She rode in silence, in deep thought. She must wrestle with this problem. Long Walker rode at her side, also in silence. He had noted and was respecting her need to think.

The young man had no way of knowing how much those thoughts concerned him. Running Eagle had planned to have a serious conversation with Long Walker to plan their future together. Now everything had changed. First her brother must be avenged.

And, she realized, there was no one else to exact this vengeance. Her grandfather, Heads Off, was old. Her own father was handicapped by his crippled leg, and her uncle, in his capacity as medicine man, was not thought of as a warrior. Owl's son was only a small child.

It became all too apparent. In all her family she was the only warrior. It must fall to her to avenge her brother, to remove the stain from the lodge of Eagle.

This would bring great changes in her life. She must abandon her thoughts and dreams of a lodge of her own. She could ride with Long Walker, but it would be as warriors together, not as husband and wife.

Running Eagle's vows of chastity as a warrior sister came back to her. She was in a state of exhaustion, weakened from her recent fast and loss of sleep the previous night. Somehow her previous vows and her present pledge of vengeance became one. She must set aside all womanly thoughts.

"Walker," the girl finally spoke in a voice tense with emotion, "you know I must avenge my brother."

Long Walker nodded sympathetically. "I know. I will help you. What must you do?"

"I do not know. The Head Splitters must feel the weight of his death."

A cold chill crept up the back of Long Walker's neck. The girl was so calm, so logical, as she announced her vow to kill Head Splitters in revenge. Such a situation was not uncommon, of course. The shocking and unnerving thing was Running Eagle's cold and direct statement. Taking her usual approach, she was driving straight ahead toward her goal.

Running Eagle did not tell him at this time about her vow of chastity. It seemed unimportant compared to the overwhelming need to devote her efforts to warrior skills and vengeance.

Late that night, long after the village was quiet, Running Eagle slipped noiselessly from her parents' lodge. She carried a small but heavy bundle, retrieved from deep behind the lodge lining.

The girl made her way among the neighboring lodges, pausing to quiet a restless horse as she passed. She came to the stream and threaded her way between scattered trees, finally emerging at a still, deep pool some distance upstream. Here she stopped and set her pack on the grass.

For a long time she stood gazing at the starry sky, silently in communion with the world and its sometimes puzzling events.

At last she knelt and opened the rawhide pack. She took out a smooth, fist-sized object and carefully tossed it into the deepest part of the pool. The resounding plunk in the still night produced an echoing plunk from a startled bullfrog in the reeds. A roosting bird fluttered sleepily, and the night was quiet again.

Methodically Running Eagle removed the rest of her carefully collected cooking stones from the pack. One at a time, the remaining stones followed the first one in a calculated, almost ritualistic ceremony. It was as if she were cutting the last ties to the life that might have been, that of a woman in her own lodge.

She discarded the last stone and stood for a moment, holding the empty rawhide pack. If anyone had been present to observe, he might have noticed that the face of the warrior woman glistened with tears in the shadowy light of the rising moon.

21

>> >> >>

During the next few moons a legend was born. Even the far-flung bands of the People gloried in the tales of the warrior woman, Running Eagle.

The story of her first experience in battle became exaggerated in the recounting almost immediately. It was forgotten that the girl had been one of the minor members of the group, a novice on her first war party. In the minds of the listeners, after a retelling or two, Running Eagle became the leader of the party. She had initiated the attack so swiftly, it was said, that while others still readied their weapons she had already struck the enemy and had killed three men.

Only slightly less exaggerated were the tales of prowess of her companion, Long Walker. At first some who heard the tale thought that the tall warrior must be her husband or lover. But no, it seemed that the girl had taken vows of chastity. Her warlike efforts were directed at avenging her brother's death. She had vowed to wreak vengeance on the Head Splitters. As a former warrior sister, she had extended her chastity. There was no clear limit to her vow—perhaps her entire lifetime, it was said. This deepened the mystery of the status of her companion, Long Walker.

Actually his status was as much a mystery to Long Walker as to anyone else. He had sought out the girl on the day after their return from the pursuit. The two took a long walk up the stream and talked of many things. Patiently the young man tried to dissuade her from her half-formed plans.

It was no use. It became apparent that she felt such a forceful call of duty that it must come before all else. She only knew that the enemy must be made to realize the folly of assault on the family of Eagle.

Long Walker exhaled a deep sigh. "Running Eagle," he said slowly, "you know that I wish you to give up this vow. I know that you are able to avenge your brother. You have proved that." He paused and sighed again. "If you must do this, I am with you." He smiled a little wistfully. "We do fight well together," he added sadly.

The decision made, it was now time to make plans. Running Eagle quickly outlined her ideas. They could follow the Head Splitters, steal horses, attack small groups, and in general harass the enemy at every opportunity.

"But Running Eagle," Long Walker protested, "this is dangerous! We cannot fight the whole Head Splitter nation!"

"So be it!" she snapped. "I will go. I did not ask your help!"

Frustrated, knowing the plan to be foolhardy, Long Walker knew also that he could not press his protest too far. If she became too angry at him she would go alone. This must not happen. He must keep his objections quiet enough to avoid angering the girl. Only in this way could he protect her from herself.

"It is good," he shrugged resignedly. "We will go."

Because Running Eagle's pledge of vengeance involved her family, the girl felt obliged to talk to her grandfather before starting her plans. That evening she approached his lodge, a little apprehensive and anxious. Heads Off had always been an impressive figure to her, dignified, calm, and aloof. She was almost afraid of him.

"Grandfather," she called, tapping on the skin lodge cover, "it is Running Eagle. I would speak with you."

In only a moment her grandmother held aside the door skin to admit the girl. The older woman embraced her briefly and motioned to a seat.

Running Eagle blinked the outside darkness from her eyes as they adjusted to the firelight. Heads Off was seated across the lodge from the doorway, reclining on his willow backrest and smoking his pipe. He nodded in recognition and waited for the girl to speak.

"Grandfather," she began hesitantly, "you know that I have been accepted into the Elk-dog Society."

He nodded, waiting for the girl to continue.

"It comes to me that there is no other warrior now in our family, since my brother's death."

Again Heads Off nodded solemnly, grieving, yet apparently puzzled.

"So," Running Eagle went on, "it falls to me to avenge him."

It seemed a long time while Heads Off took three deliberate puffs on his fragrant pipe. She watched the blue-white smoke rise toward the hole at the lodge's apex. Finally Heads Off spoke slowly.

"My daughter, I thought him avenged already. You would do more?"

"Yes, Grandfather."

"What? How long?"

Rapidly she sketched out her plan—the harassment, ambush, horse stealing. "I would make the Head Splitters regret and repay the debt to our family."

The chief nodded again. "This would be very dangerous."

"Yes, Grandfather, but it must be. I have vowed vengeance. Long Walker goes with me."

"*Aiee!* I do not know." Heads Off shook his head in apparent confusion. He turned to his wife.

"Tall One! Is this the custom of the People? It would not be done in my own tribe."

Once again Running Eagle was startled to recall that her grandfather had originally been an outsider. He seemed so much a part of the People now.

"Not usual, but not unheard of, my husband." Tall One had always called him "my husband" since their marriage, so long ago now. "There was a warrior woman, long ago, who led the People, before we came south."

That, Heads Off knew, was many generations ago, when the tribe still ranged the northern plains. The story was a dim legend, recounted with their creation story.

"Of course," Tall One continued, "you know that some women go with their husbands on hunts and raids."

Heads Off sighed deeply. That was different than the path of vengeance set forth by young Running Eagle.

The girl sat, watching him closely. The approval of the band chief was not absolutely necessary, but she valued it highly. As she studied his face, she was suddenly impressed with the fact that her grandfather looked old and tired. Of course, she thought, the grief is his, too, over Bobcat's loss.

Now Heads Off partially rose to take down from its place of honor the Spanish bit, talisman of his medicine. He held it reverently in the firelight, sparkling reflections darting from the silver ornaments like shining minnows in a clear stream. Gently he held it toward her.

"Here, Daughter. Use it in your mission."

Running Eagle was astonished. It was beyond belief that Heads Off would entrust her with this most powerful of medicines, the Elk-dog medicine of the People. It was this revered object which had originally helped them to control the horse.

"Grandfather," she stammered, "I cannot. Suppose I am killed, and the Elk-dog medicine lost." She must not, she realized, place her vengeance above the importance to the tribe of this most powerful of medicines. "Let it remain here. I will still draw strength from it."

Cautiously she extended a hand, touching the rings, the shiny bangles. She had never before touched the object. The smooth, shiny surfaces were still warm from the heat of the afternoon sun. She could feel the warmth, the strength, flowing into her fingertips.

Yes, she could not risk the loss of this important symbol of the Elk-dog band. It must stay here.

22
≫ ≫ ≫

Some time later a small hunting party of Head Splitters camped near a stream called Oak River by their tribe. They had killed no game and had not even searched too hard. It was a teaching mission for three of the younger hunters. In this way the young men would learn to track, to stand sentry, and to ride long distances. Some day these skills would stand them in good stead as mature warriors.

The two leaders of the party had spread their robes, assigning the night watch to young Woodpecker. It was his first watch, but there was little danger. They were only a day's travel from the main camp.

The horses were hobbled in the grassy bend of the stream, and they placidly grazed. Black Fox took a last look around, advised the youngsters near the fire to get some rest, and sought his bed. His companion was already snoring.

Woodpecker sat on a stone at the edge of the meadow. It was still warm from the sun and felt good against his skin, where the top edge of his leggings only partially covered his buttocks.

The night was dark, but soon there would be a moon, only a little past full. Still, it was lonely here on watch. The familiar night sounds were comforting, but he found himself thinking strange, anxious thoughts. What if, by some mischance, a man on watch were killed at his post? It was said that his spirit, attempting to cross over in the darkness, would become lost and wander forever in the black space between worlds. Woodpecker shivered a little and slid down further against his boulder. He was not afraid, of course, only cautious.

He wondered if there were any disembodied spirits wandering near this spot. Anxiously he studied the dark fringe of timber along the stream.

The first light of the rising moon revealed the dim shapes of the horses in the meadow. They were moving nervously. Woodpecker was hesitant to sound the alarm. He waited a long time, finally assuring himself that something or someone was disturbing the animals.

Silently he slipped along a shallow draw toward the meadow, pausing to look occasionally. The horses were bunching together and moving in a southerly direction, as if they were being cautiously herded away from the camp.

The orange rim of the moon rose higher, and now he could see the ghostly form of a tall rider carefully driving the horses before him.

"The horses!" Woodpecker yelled. "They are stealing the horses!"

The sleeping forms at the fire sprang to their feet, and instantly Woodpecker was aware of the vibrating twang of a bowstring somewhere in the area. One of the sleepily stumbling figures crumpled, falling almost into the fire. Another twang, and yet another.

Then came a rumble of hooves, and the horse herd came running almost directly at him, urged by the shouts of the tall rider. They thundered past, and the warrior paused briefly, holding a spotted horse by the rein. From somewhere in the tall grass a slim figure, apparently the hidden bowman, vaulted into the saddle. The two raced out of sight after the disappearing horse herd.

Woodpecker ran quickly to the fire, calling out in alarm. Only a single figure rose to greet him.

"Woodpecker? Is it you?" Black Fox called.

"Yes! The horses are gone!"

"I know."

"Where are the others?"

"All dead."

"I am sorry, Fox. I failed at the watch!"

"No, Woodpecker. You gave the alarm."

"But too late!"

Black Fox shook his head. "You were against skilled warriors. The attack was well planned. Did you see them?"

Woodpecker nodded. "A tall man on a dark horse. A bowman in the grass. The first man led a horse for the other."

"Yes, I saw that one."

He was silent a long time before he spoke again. "Woodpecker, I know these two. I have met them before."

Thus it happened that the legend of dread Crazy Woman was born among the Head Splitters. In the following moons she and her companion, the tall warrior, seemed to be everywhere. They struck an isolated hunting camp, a small war party, they drove away horses, usually at night. This was the most fearsome thing to a people for whom dying in the darkness was repugnant and hazardous. The two raiders struck swiftly and disappeared like ghosts in the mists of the night, leaving behind the dead and dying.

More sentries were posted, but sentries appeared to be the favorite victims of Crazy Woman.

The motive of the two raiders was soon known. One of the young men who were spared in an early skirmish had been told, so that her victims might know. The warrior woman fought to avenge her brother, who had been killed by Head Splitters. In symbolism her raids were always carried out on her brother's horse, an ugly mouse-colored animal with white splashes across the rump. Her deadly companion, skilled with lance, knife, and club, rode a powerful dark stallion.

The ghostly pair seemed to be everywhere. In one night when mist lay heavy on the prairie, they were reported in at least three areas, each a day's journey apart from the other two. It was whispered that they were somehow not of this world.

Black Fox was not convinced. He had seen the original charge of Crazy Woman and had seen her at close distance. There was nothing supernatural about her, he knew. This was a woman of flesh and bone and blood. She must be stopped. She was killing the finest young warriors of his tribe.

Black Fox had one major dilemma in all this. Having seen the girl, he was convinced that she was the most beautiful woman he had ever imagined in his wildest dreams. Now he was confused. She was the focal point of all his waking thoughts, but he was unsure whether he wished to possess her or to kill her. He was certain that it must be one or the other. Perhaps both.

There must be a way to draw her out, to make her vulnerable to defeat or capture. Black Fox knew he must devise a clever plan, for the two were formidable warriors. He had seen them in action twice, now, both times to his dismay.

If he could entice the warrior woman and her companion out and away from their territory, he thought, then their unfamiliarity with the terrain would place them at a disadvantage. A complicated scheme began to form in his mind.

23

>> >> >>

The exploits of Running Eagle were perhaps less known to her own people than to the enemy. It was known that the girl and her ever-present companion, Long Walker, were constantly going on some obscure war party. The two would return, quietly state their deeds at the warriors' circle, and be gone again.

There were some who listened with a degree of disbelief as they recited their honors and kills of the enemy. Of course it was difficult *not* to believe when the pair returned driving bands of captured horses. The personal herds of Running Eagle and Long Walker increased constantly.

Yet even with many fine animals to choose from, Running Eagle continued to ride the rawboned gelding, Owl Dung. It was understood by the People that this was a part of her vows to avenge her brother. The horse had been his, so it now carried his avenger.

As to the rest of her vows, there was little agreement. It was said that she remained celibate, and this observation was strengthened by the attitude of Long

Walker. The young man appeared devoted and loyal, but he was obviously frustrated. This also led to much speculation about the duration of Running Eagle's vows of vengeance. She appeared no nearer the fulfillment of her purpose than she had ever been.

This was a constant concern to her friend Long Walker. Initially he had hoped that her thirst for vengeance would weaken, that she would begin to see her purpose accomplished. He attempted to encourage this view as much as he dared, praising each success and implying that surely now Bobcat was avenged. Finally Running Eagle spoke to him sternly.

"Walker, I will say when it is over! Until then, I ride against the Head Splitters."

Walker nodded helplessly. "And I ride with you?"

"Of course!"

She flashed him the dazzling smile which had come to make their relationship all the more painful. She nudged Owl Dung in the ribs and moved forward to drive their newly captured horses toward the camp.

Aiee, Long Walker mused. She enjoys this too much. He had sometimes seen her large dark eyes flash like real-fire as she prepared an attack. The ripple of her laughter as they sorted and divided the spoils of a raid was like a knife in his heart.

Still, the laughter was for him and for the things they shared. Long Walker only wished that they could share much more. It was difficult to be content with their companionship and their effort together as a fighting unit.

Long Walker had to admit, of course, that their skill as warriors was a thing of great pleasure to him. Their success was a thing in which to take pride. No one, he thought, could remember a more effective fighting team, their skills so perfectly complemented to each other. Bow, lance, war club, knife, skill with Elk-dogs— all were a part of their combined approach. Running Eagle's strategy was often so imaginative, so well fitted to the customs and habits of the enemy as well as to their own skills, that he never ceased to marvel.

The girl had an uncanny ability to evaluate a situation and utilize everything to her advantage.

Gradually his cautious arguments after each encounter weakened, and the two assumed a stable relationship. Long Walker still clung to the dream of an end to the girl's campaign, but it became easier to postpone. He gloried in their time together, exclusively with each other. They talked of many things. They teased, laughed, rode, ate, and slept.

Sometimes they even snuggled together for warmth against the chill of the prairie night. This was most frustrating of all for Long Walker. He longed to hold the girl as a man holds a woman, in the fulfillment of marriage. Yet he knew that he must not. Even if he were able to persuade her, he would be guilty of breaking one of the strongest customs of the People. To encourage another to break a sacred vow would be extremely bad medicine.

So their relationship grew and prospered in this strange way. They became more and more a part of each other, even though kept apart by the vows of Running Eagle.

The two had stopped to trade for supplies with some Growers, several sleeps from their own band, when they learned of a new development.

"You are Running Eagle?" the woman asked as she offered her dried corn for the meat they had brought.

Long Walker answered with another question. "What do you know of Running Eagle?"

"That she brings vengeance against the Head Splitters."

The woman's attitude was completely noncommittal. The Growers traded freely with all comers and considered themselves entirely neutral. Only so could they survive in permanent locations amid the various warlike nomads of the plains.

"Some young men were here looking for you," she continued.

Instantly Running Eagle was alert. "Head Splitters?"

"No, no, your own tribe."

"What did they want?"

"They wished to ride with you, to ride against the Head Splitters."

Running Eagle was confused. It had not occurred to her that her campaign was more than a private foray. That young warriors would seek her out to follow as their leader was a new idea, and somewhat flattering.

"Where are they now?"

The woman shrugged. "Who knows about young men? We told them where your People are camped."

"You *told* them? They are not of our band?"

"No. Theirs is the band of a chief called Rides-the-Wind." She pointed northeast.

"The *Northern* band?" Long Walker interjected. "How did they know of Running Eagle?"

The woman smiled. "Everyone on the plains knows of Running Eagle. The Head Splitters talk much of her. They call her Crazy Woman, but they are afraid."

Embarrassed, the woman became silent, as if she had said too much and violated her position of neutrality.

Excited yet puzzled, the two left the Growers and set their trail for the camp of their own band. This was becoming a far bigger thing than it seemed at first.

"Would you let them ride with us, Running Eagle?"

"I do not know. I think not. But, *aiee*, we could lead a raid they would remember for their grandchildren to hear of!"

She looked straight ahead, but Long Walker saw that there was an excited glitter in her eyes. The old feeling of alarm came creeping back as he recognized the sign. It was the way she looked when she was planning her attack strategy.

Long Walker said nothing, but his heart became heavy. It was not good. He did not wish to see her so pleased and excited over the prospect of a major campaign. Again came the warning thought, the feeling that she was enjoying all this too much for her own good.

Where would it all end? With the death or capture of Running Eagle? There was little to make Long Walker feel otherwise.

24
>> >> >>

Running Eagle and Long Walker topped the last rise and looked down on the Elk-dog band's summer camp. For some time they had seen the gray haze of smoke from cooking fires as it hung near the horizon.

The riders paused for a moment to observe the scattered lodges in the meadow near the river. Something had changed remarkably since their most recent departure, a few suns ago.

"*Aiee,*" observed Long Walker, "the band has grown!"

The loosely organized bands of the People varied constantly in size and composition. Basically they were formed around a respected chief and his family's friends and relatives. Still, there was a constant shifting of allegiance. Good fortune or misfortune to a band might cause a few warriors to move with their families to join another group for a season.

Of course some ne'er-do-wells constantly remained disgruntled at their status and changed their alliance nearly every summer. These were not a special asset to the band, and little was expected of them.

On the other hand, able warriors or adventurous young men might choose to spend a season with the band of a popular chief or subchief. The shifting fortunes of political prestige, admiration for a chief's reputation, or merely a search for adventure with an aggressive leader might be motives.

Now the returning warriors noted that the increase in the size of the band was largely in the bend of the stream, to the west of the main camp. Running Eagle observed that the dwellings were of brush; they were temporary summer shelters. That would mean that these were probably young warriors seeking excitement. There were no families with them. For a moment she wondered what had been occurring in the Elk-dog band to attract such a following.

At that moment the two riders were sighted from below, and a great shout went up. A number of men leaped to their horses and rushed to meet the newcomers.

They streamed across the meadow and up the slope with reckless abandon, singing, shouting, and performing feats of daring horsemanship to attract attention. Snatches and partial phrases of their jubilant cries began to be distinguishable.

"—has struck the enemy to hurt him—"

"—feared by all Head Splitters—"

"—mightiest of warriors—"

"—we ride with Running Eagle!"

The girl's mouth dropped open in astonishment. Here were at least twenty young warriors swearing allegiance to her as leader. She glanced at Long Walker, only to see his face darkly marked by displeasure. Her own feelings were mixed. She could not help but feel flattered, yet something in her resented interference. Her vows of vengeance had been a private, a personal thing. Somehow this public adulation was a threat to her.

Now the young men were surrounding the pair, still singing, some voicing the full-throated war cry of the People. They moved on toward the camp. Children ran to meet the party, accompanied by yapping dogs. Excitement was high.

It was some time before Running Eagle could tear herself away from her admirers and make her way to the lodge of her parents. There she spent a pleasant interlude, exchanging news while her mother prepared food. Most exciting, of course, was the talk of her growing band of followers.

Young warriors had been arriving almost daily, her father related. Most were from the Northern band, closest of the other groups. Some, however, were from the Mountain and the Red Rocks bands. There were many family ties with these groups. Two young men had come all the way from the Eastern band, known for its eccentric behavior and different customs.

"What do you think of all this, Father?"

Eagle spread upturned palms in a broad shrug of puzzlement. "Who knows, Daughter? When has such a thing happened before?"

Not since Heads Off brought the first Elk-dog, both knew. Young men and older men with families had gravitated toward this, the Southern band. That was when the name change occurred, because of the special circumstances. It had become the most prestigious of the bands and had been called the Elk-dog band ever since. So important was the acquisition of the horse that often the entire tribe was now called the Elk-dog People by other groups.

Running Eagle was still confused by her conflicting emotions. "But what should I do?"

"Whatever you wish. I think they would follow you anywhere."

"Would that take power from our chiefs?"

"I think not, Eagle Woman."

The girl elected not to notice her father's use of her former name.

"Their authority is a different thing," he continued. "It is for the entire band. If you do not break any of the council's rules, who is to care?"

Long Walker, when he came by after darkness had

fallen, was much more pessimistic. The two strolled along the stream in silence for a time, then stopped to talk. They were very near the spot where the girl had discarded her cooking stones.

"Running Eagle, you must stop this thing!"

It was the first time he had spoken so for some time, and she was instantly defensive.

"What do you mean?"

"Tell the young men to go home."

"I will decide that," she snapped. "They come to follow me!"

"But, Eagle," he pleaded. "These are thrill seekers. They will not be good warriors."

"Are you afraid their skill is greater than yours?" she taunted.

"No, no." He shook his head. "It is only that now you can never be alone. Anywhere you go, you will be followed by these young men. You cannot fulfill your vows, because they will be interfering. Give it up, Running Eagle. You have killed enough Head Splitters."

In her heart she knew that he was right, but she was furious that he would attempt to convince her. Angrily she turned on him.

"Walker, you cannot tell me when my vows are fulfilled," she almost screamed at him. "If you do not wish to ride with me, there are many who do!"

She stumbled away in the night, glad that the darkness hid the glisten of tears on her cheeks. Why had she treated her friend this way? Each time, it seemed, that they were on the verge of becoming close, something happened to spoil it.

Suddenly an idea occurred to her. She would go and talk to Owl. Her uncle had always been able to give understanding and advice.

She turned aside, made her way among the lodges, and finally stopped before the medicine man's dwelling. She tapped on the taut skin lodge cover.

"Uncle," she called, "it is Running Eagle!"

Willow drew back the door skin for the girl to enter and beckoned her inside. It was late, time to retire, but the couple knew that the young relative had a need.

Running Eagle glanced at young Rabbit, already sleeping peacefully on a pile of robes. The girl turned back to her uncle. Owl sat smoking, relaxed, waiting. He had some idea what was bothering the young woman but waited to hear.

"Uncle, you must help me!" she blurted.

Rapidly her story poured forth, venting all the frustration and dilemma. Not all, perhaps. She omitted how badly she wanted to go to Long Walker for comfort and companionship. She did not understand how she could make decisions without hesitation in combat but not in her life.

Owl was silent a long time, but finally spoke. "Daughter, these choices are yours. All that you say is true. These young men are thrill seekers. They would follow you, but their judgment might not be the best." He paused for a moment in reflection, then injected a cautious question. "What does Long Walker say?"

"That does not matter," she answered irritably. "It is my decision."

Owl nodded. "True. You must decide."

His question had been answered.

"Running Eagle, you have surely avenged your brother. Your deeds are known across the whole prairie. So you could do as you wish. No one will think less of you if you send your followers home. But," he shrugged, "it is your choice."

Though his words were noncommittal, Running Eagle felt that a great weight had been lifted from her shoulders. In effect she had received approval from someone outside the immediate situation. She could now do as her heart was telling her.

The girl rose, thanked the two warmly, and gently patted the sleeping Rabbit on the head. Now she knew what she must do. She slipped outside and paused for a moment to allow her eyes to become accustomed to the darkness. Then she would go in search of Long

Walker. In her mind he would still be where she left him beside the deep pool, sad and depressed. She smiled to herself in the darkness. Walker would be so pleased at her decision.

In the distance there was the sound of an approaching horse. She listened, evaluating the hoofbeats. The rider was in a great hurry, and the animal was tired, pushed almost to exhaustion.

The newcomer called out and, apparently by coincidence, wandered into the temporary camp of the outsiders. There was excited talk, then shouts and the sounds of running feet, and people came hurrying into the main camp. Running Eagle could catch only portions of the confused shouting.

"—Northern band attacked—"

"—Head Splitters—"

"—go and help them "

"*Where is Running Eagle?*"

The girl realized the situation with a sinking heart. She would be expected to lead a war party to help the Northern band. It was too late for the choice she had been considering, for now there was none.

Frustrated, Running Eagle felt again the helpless sensation she had experienced earlier in the summer. Somehow there had been set in motion a series of events over which she had no control.

She had no choice. There had never been one.

25
>> >> >>

Again Running Eagle and Long Walker rode side by side, this time headed north. Behind them straggled some thirty warriors, noisy, singing, chanting, or aimlessly racing their horses back and forth. She could hardly believe all the events of the past day.

She had arrived home, expecting to rest and, at leisure, to decide whether to go out on another foray. Then she had learned of the impromptu gathering of her young followers and had had her argument with Long Walker over it. Just as she had felt that she had these problems resolved in her own mind, the messenger had arrived from the Northern band.

This was the most disconcerting happening of all. The Northern band had been struck by a large force of Head Splitters, moving somewhat outside their usual territory. A number of the People had been killed, and Rides-the-Wind himself was wounded but was expected to recover.

Most alarming, however, was the manner in which the attack had been planned—coolly and efficiently.

The invaders had captured two young men, apparently for the sole purpose of releasing them later. The two had been instructed to carry a message to their chiefs.

This raid had but one purpose—to punish the People for the depredations of Running Eagle. The enemy had referred to her as Crazy Woman, but there was no doubt as to whom they meant.

The Head Splitters had also left no doubt that they intended to raid again and would continue to do so until the forays of Crazy Woman ceased.

The exhausted messenger had come not to plead with the girl to stop, but to ask her help. With a force of warriors, he pleaded, they could pursue and punish the enemy war party. But they must move quickly, before the Head Splitters left the area.

A hasty council was called. It had been decided that Running Eagle would lead a war party of volunteers, to include those who had declared themselves her followers. Most of the warriors of the Elk-dog band would remain behind. There was the strong possibility that the entire plan by the enemy was designed to draw the fighting men away from the camp. Then a surprise strike on the defenseless band would be devastating.

So it had been decided. Even without those young men who elected to go on the war party, the band that stayed at the camp remained nearly at full strength. Running Eagle would have over thirty warriors, a strong force in itself.

There had been no question as to who would lead the war party. Running Eagle had been challenged, and it was her right to lead the answering force. Indeed, her duty.

Things moved rapidly, and by daylight the avenging force was ready to depart. Running Eagle was pleased and relieved when Long Walker approached on his big bay.

"I still ride with you?"

"Of course!"

She flashed the dazzling smile that always made

Long Walker's heart pound in his chest, and the two led the procession out into the prairie. The two horses, familiar by long association, instinctively moved together as they walked. The knees of the riders occasionally touched, and the nearness of Long Walker was comforting to the girl.

They talked as they rode. Both were concerned that the majority of their followers were undisciplined and inexperienced. A few warriors from their own band had skill, knowledge, and experience, but the others left much to be desired. They cavorted senselessly, abused horses that might need to be in top condition, and uselessly expended themselves. Long Walker was disgusted.

It would be necessary, the two leaders decided, to choose a couple of responsible-appearing warriors from the group and ask them to help in controlling the more exuberant novices. One such man was a quiet youth named Flying Squirrel. When the time came for night camp, they decided, it would be time to approach him and perhaps others to initiate some semblance of discipline and order.

Meanwhile it might even be useful for some of the more emotionally tense young warriors to tire themselves out a little. Running Eagle did not think that it was her place to criticize too much. After all, on her first war party she had broken custom in the now famous charge that had resulted in all this. From a novice warrior, she had become, to the enemy, Crazy Woman, scourge of the plains.

She could not help but be proud of her accomplishments, even as she wished sometimes that she had never aspired to warrior status. She glanced back at the motley straggle behind her and shook her head.

At least all of her would-be warriors showed some rudimentary knowledge of behavior. So far, none had ridden ahead of her and Walker. If that happened, it was time to stop and take firm steps.

But such a thing did not happen. The members of the party, even the foolish ones, observed the common courtesy, and a good day's travel resulted. By the time Sun Boy stood low in the west, Running Eagle felt somewhat better. It would be two, maybe three sleeps before they made contact with the Head Splitters. By that time the war party might well be more organized and disciplined.

For now they would stop somewhat before dark. They had covered much distance and were moving into unfamiliar territory. The prairie ahead looked rougher and more hilly. This was verified by the men of the Northern band who had been this way before.

So a halt was called, and campfires began to blossom as the light of Sun Boy's torch faded. This would be the last camp where fires would be permitted, but for now the enemy would be at least two sleeps away.

Long Walker strolled around the camp and requested Flying Squirrel and two others to meet at the fire of Running Eagle. It was time to begin some sort of organization.

26

>> >> >>

Black Fox sat, waiting. There was nothing else to do at the moment. He could hardly contain his enthusiasm, but he knew that he must, so he forcibly called upon himself to relax. With conscious effort he softened his tense muscles and stretched full-length on a robe spread over a level patch of short buffalo grass.

He arranged his position so he could watch the distant prairie. If he had planned correctly, today would be the time. And his plan was working well.

Black Fox had been preoccupied all summer with thoughts of the warrior woman. Crazy though she might be, she was the most beautiful woman he had ever seen.

He devised and then rejected several plans to capture her. None were quite satisfactory, or they involved too much risk, or they would reveal too much about his own feelings for this woman of the enemy.

He had decided that it must be a capture. Never had he wanted to possess a woman as much as he did this one. To kill her would be a waste. He could take her to his lodge, and if she became a docile wife, so be it. If not, if it appeared dangerous to keep her alive, she could easily be killed at any time.

Meanwhile the warrior woman was dangerous to his tribe. Every few sleeps, it seemed, there was news of another raid by Crazy Woman. She struck mostly at night, it was said, when the danger to the spirit of a dying warrior was at its greatest. An arrow precisely aimed at a sentry, a few horses stolen, harassment at every turn.

And always the stories were the same. There were but two attackers, Crazy Woman and her ever-present companion, the tall warrior. Black Fox wondered about the relationship of these two. Was this the girl's husband?

It was no matter, Black Fox decided. After he captured the girl, she would become his wife. The other man, whatever his status, could be disposed of in any one of a number of ways. It might be interesting to keep the man alive for a while, to try to see what attracted his beautiful companion.

But for now, any plan to capture the two was unquestionably dangerous. Black Fox had seen these two in action and respected their skill with weapons. In addition, the woman apparently had no fear. That alone would make her unpredictable and dangerous.

Finally Black Fox began to develop a plan. The more he considered, the more it seemed workable. If it were successful, it would serve several desirable purposes. It would rid the plains of the dangerous pair, and the hunters could again search for buffalo in safety.

Success would bring him fame and prestige as a rising young subchief. The impact of this prestige could not be overlooked as it related to his political career.

Most important of all, however, was the motive he would share with no one. Black Fox admitted only to himself the driving force behind his need to resolve the matter of Crazy Woman. It was the all-absorbing need to possess this girl. He thought again and again of the brief time he had seen her. He could picture in his mind's eye her spectacular charge, the supple curves of her body as she fought, and her graceful balance on the horse. The burning message of hate as their eyes met for a moment had only served to fix his attention further. Black Fox admired a horse or a woman with spirit. It became only a greater challenge to find a way to break that spirit.

His immediate plan for the defeat and capture of Crazy Woman was based around one single fact. It had become more apparent as time passed that her entire motive was vengeance. Revenge for the loss of a brother, it was said.

Now, reasoned Black Fox, if her thoughts revolved around revenge, let it be used against her. If some incident could be created that Crazy Woman would see as a personal affront, it might affect her judgment.

It must be a bold attack against her tribe. Not against her own band, Black Fox thought, but one of the others. That would draw her out, make her fight in unfamiliar territory. After long thought, he had decided on the Northern band.

It was no problem to recruit young men for a prolonged war party into enemy territory. His main difficulty was to select only the best and most reliable warriors. In a short while Black Fox had assembled a group of his tribe's finest, ready to follow this popular leader.

Now it became a matter of quietly observing the Northern band while Black Fox and his followers familiarized themselves with the features of the terrain. One of the critical elements of the plan was that the presence of an invading war party not be suspected until the proper moment.

Eventually that moment had come. When a large number of the men of the Northern band had gone on a hunt, Black Fox and his raiders swooped down on the village. Even so, it was difficult for a time. The few warriors left in camp defended fiercely, and the attackers had been hurt.

They had carried off two boys, carefully instructed them by means of sign language, and released them to tell the purpose of the raid. Then the raiding party had openly headed southwest toward its own territory. As Black Fox had expected, a messenger soon set forth to the south. All members of the war party had been cautioned not to stop him, not to even show themselves.

The messenger took exactly the route expected. Straight to the south, following a buffalo trail as old as the earth itself, the messenger rode. The plan was working well. Black Fox and all his raiders followed, well behind, still taking care not to be seen.

He had already selected the spot for the ambush. A cleft in a range of the rolling hills narrowed the buffalo trail, as a stream narrows through the rocks. At this point Crazy Woman would have no room to maneuver, to use her skill with the horse. Warriors would strike from hiding, and their quarry could be taken quickly.

Black Fox stirred from his pleasant reverie as he saw an approaching rider hurrying from the south. Impatiently he rose and waited while the scout crossed the valley. At times horse and rider were lost from sight in the tall, waving expanse of real-grass. Finally the scout ascended the ridge and stood before him.

"They come! There are about thirty. They will be here," he paused to point upward, "when the sun is there."

Thirty. More than he had expected. But no matter. They would be forced to spread out in a long line, to make their way through the pass. The warriors of Black Fox could strike the unsuspecting party in the middle, cut them in two, and separate them from their leaders.

"It is good," he told the scout. "Come."

The two made their way back to where the rest of the war party waited in concealment. Young men rose to their feet, picking up their weapons in eagerness.

"They come," announced Black Fox. "There are thirty, so we must do well."

A murmur rippled around the group, but Black Fox signaled for silence again.

"Let the leaders come well through the pass before we show ourselves. They will not expect us to be in this area. We are only one sleep from their own camp."

Black Fox paused a moment, then added a last reminder. "Remember, the Crazy Woman and her man are not to be harmed. Shoot their horses if necessary, but I want those two alive!"

27

>> >> >>

Running Eagle had a bad feeling as they approached the narrow cleft in the hills. She wished that Owl had been able to give them a better prediction. Apparently the medicine man had not been able to see a clear vision for the journey.

"Only be very careful, Running Eagle. This is a dangerous mission," Owl had said.

She had nodded and moved on to other things in preparation for leaving, but now his remarks took on new importance.

It could be seen that this was dangerous country. The broken slopes, the vast expanses of real-grass, and the thick, nodding meadows of plume grass furnished endless places of concealment for warriors. At this time of the season, both of these grasses grew taller than a man's head. To remain still almost anywhere was to be hidden.

It was good, she reflected, that the Head Splitters were not in this immediate area. The range of hills ahead would afford an ideal ambush. But, following the raid, the attackers had been observed to ride rapidly southwest. An effort, no doubt, to escape the certain retaliation of the People. It would be necessary to track the retreating enemy and overtake them.

But for now, the enemy was far away. It would be perhaps two more sleeps before they located the trail. And that was good. The exuberant young men were somewhat better behaved today, due to the efforts of Flying Squirrel and the others.

Still, Running Eagle had misgivings. She would have much preferred to travel alone with Long Walker, harassing the enemy and striking the sentries by night. Again she felt the frustration of having been forced against her will into a pattern of events which she could not control. She did not like the way the pattern was developing. Ahead seemed ever more of the wrong direction, and she was powerless to stop it. She wished to break free of the relentlessly threatening series of events, to shout stop, and to ride away in carefree companionship with Long Walker.

She had reveled in their friendship, their time together, but not enough, she now realized. She should have treasured it so highly that she could never have let it go, no matter what the cost.

Now she sometimes thought of herself as a person in a tale of long ago, retold around the story fires. The outcome was already certain, and there was no way to change it. She was living out the story as it unfolded but still had no knowledge of its outcome. She wondered if Long Walker felt this frustration as she did. She thought so.

"Walker," she spoke casually, avoiding her real concern, "will these men be ready when we fight?"

"I think so. They are new at battle but they are brave." He was quiet a moment and then spoke again. "Just now I am thinking about the ridge ahead."

"You, too? Why?"

"It is a perfect place for ambush."

The girl nodded. "True. But the Head Splitters are far away to the west."

"But if they were not, Running Eagle?"

She nodded again. "It would be the place."

She halted and raised her hand. "We go through the pass with care. Stay close together. Walker and I go first. Watch the hillside."

Briskly the two rode forward to pass the danger area rapidly. There was nothing. Not a seed stalk moved among the tall grasses, and there was complete silence.

Running Eagle was well past the danger spot before she realized that the silence was wrong. There should have been the sounds of the prairie everywhere. The song of a meadowlark, the scream of a hawk overhead, the rustle of a deer feeding on the hillside, perhaps.

She drew rein and signaled Long Walker to silence. "Walker! It is too quiet."

At that moment came a muffled sound from behind the shoulder of the hill. It was an odd, unnatural sound, and it could have resulted from only one source. It was a partly choked snort, the sound a horse can still make when its muzzle has been tied with a thong to prevent its calling out.

Running Eagle turned to shout the warning, but she was too late. With the terrifying falsetto war cry of the Head Splitters, warriors rose from hiding all along the sides of the pass, from behind every rock, from the ground itself, it seemed. They fought on foot, ducking and dodging among the horses.

"Straight ahead!" the girl shouted. "The stream."

She jammed heels into the ribs of the startled Owl Dung, and he sprang into a dead run. The scattered timber ahead would allow them to organize a stand for defense.

There were pounding hooves behind her, and she risked a glance. Two of her young warriors followed closely, but there was no sign of Long Walker.

Without a moment's thought, the girl pulled the gelding to a sliding stop, pivoted, and charged back toward the pass. There was a moment to assess the situation while she raced back. Her party had been cut in two, with several dead or injured lying in the mouth of the pass. The fight still raged beyond, but she could see nothing.

Long Walker's horse was down, and he was scrambling free to stand ready to fight. Except for the two now riding with her, no others had come through the pass alive.

"Walker!" she yelled, not knowing whether he heard or not.

Enemy warriors were running toward him as she thundered toward the spot. The horse made a quick, catlike turn around the lone figure, and as the animal dropped his hips to pivot, Long Walker swung up behind the girl.

One of the young men with Running Eagle gave a triumphant yell and an obscene gesture as he turned. He was met by a shower of arrows and dropped from the saddle like a stone. The horse ran loose, confused, reins trailing. There was no time to catch the animal for Long Walker.

Another flight of arrows whistled past, and Owl Dung screamed with pain and rage and ran faster. They had reached the trees before mounted enemy warriors began to stream across the meadow in pursuit.

Escape now appeared impossible. The three fugitives could in no way defend themselves against the entire war party of Head Splitters. But they could not run with one horse forced to carry double.

There was a low cough at her elbow, and Running Eagle glanced aside. The young warrior who had stayed by her side was breathing heavily, blood trickling from the corner of his mouth. The feathered end of an arrow shaft protruded from near the center of his chest. His eyes were glazing as Long Walker sprang to help him from his horse.

By the time Walker had deposited the dying youth as gently as possible on the grass, his breath was coming in bubbling, irregular gasps. Running Eagle caught the rein of the horse. The young warrior would have no further use for it now. She handed the rein to Long Walker, and the two stepped into the partial shelter of the streambed, leading the horses. One last chance had opened to them. With two horses they would have at least a chance to evade the enemy pursuit.

If only the enemy would delay a charge at the strip of woods for a short while, they might have a chance to escape down the streambed.

Running Eagle thought sadly of the youth who had provided their chance at escape, however slim. He had done so at the cost of his own life.

She was embarrassed and depressed that she could not even remember the young man's name.

28

≫ ≫ ≫

The two fugitives huddled together in the twilight, waiting for full darkness to come. There was little chance of the enemy's risking a fight in the darkness. They would use the hours of darkness to travel.

There was no doubt that they would be followed, and among the Head Splitters were excellent trackers. The goal would be to put enough distance between themselves and the trackers to make their escape.

Running Eagle and Long Walker had left the stream the moment that the shouts behind indicated the discovery of the disappearance. They rode as rapidly as possible for a time, finally pausing in a rough and rocky canyon to hide and rest. They concealed the horses in a brushy draw, then hid themselves in another, where the tall plume grass offered concealment. Owl Dung's wound proved to be a minor one—a long gash across the rump, probably made by a sharp flint arrowhead.

Evening was near, and they had only to hide until dark, when the Head Splitters would stop the search until morning. Three times they had heard the sounds of searching warriors. Each time they huddled against the stone wall of the canyon while the rider searched on the rim above them, looking down into their hiding place. Only the slight overhang of the ledge kept them from sight of the searchers. Several times shouts in the distance caused momentary uneasiness.

During the intervals between threatened discovery, they talked quietly or watched the day lengthen toward night. Both were more optimistic now; time was on their side. As if in good omen, a large flock of honking geese moved high over their hiding place in a long line. The birds were migrating, heading due south for the coming winter. The fugitives watched and listened in silence, until the birds were long out of sight and only the faint resonance of their cries was heard.

Just before dark a thin cloud bank moved across the prairie, and a scatter of light rain began to fall.

"It is good," observed Walker. "It will help to cover our trail."

Good though it might be, the cold rain chilled to the bone. The two huddled together for warmth, only partially sheltered by the overhanging rock.

"We could build a fire," Long Walker joked.

Both chuckled. Then their eyes met in amazement.

"We could, Walker! Light it just before we leave. It would be morning before they discover it was a trick."

Both moved quietly to collect fuel in the gathering darkness. They laid out a long and narrow pile of wood along the base of the rock. At one end a pack rat's nest of dry twigs would make a hot, smokeless blaze. After burning for some time, the flames would encounter larger, greener fuel to produce a big smoky fire. The Head Splitters would suspect a trick, of course, but it would take time to prove it. Meanwhile the fugitives would be on their way. They settled back down to wait. Darkness came slowly under the cloud cover, the light robe of Rain Maker.

"Walker, I have wondered. Why do you think this has happened?"

"Why has what happened?"

"That we are alive. They could have killed us both, easily. Those beside us were killed."

Long Walker had wondered this, also. After his horse was struck there was a time when he lay there help-less, a leg pinned under the dying stallion. It should have been easy to kill him then, either by arrows or with the deadly stone clubs. Yet he had been spared. He shook his head.

"I do not know. But do you remember the young chief who rode away, after the fight on your first war party? I saw him today."

"Young chief? The handsome one?"

Long Walker gave her a quick, resentful look. "I do not know of that, Eagle, but he is the same one."

"But who is he? What does he want?"

Running Eagle had some idea, already. She remem-bered the last, intense look as Black Fox rode away, the look of a man who wishes to kill but is prevented. Yet there was something else. There had been, inter-mingled, the admiring look of a man who covets a woman.

Even at the time, in the heat of the fight, there had been the momentary recognition, a feel of excitement mixed with revulsion. She had thought of it since, from time to time.

"I can only think," Long Walker was answering, "that he wants us alive for some purpose."

The two looked at each other in partial understand-ing that made their bewilderment even more frustrat-ing. Neither voiced the gnawing suspicions, ones they were scarcely able to admit to themselves.

Both were thinking, of course, of the long-recognized desire of the enemy for girls of the People. "Our women are prettier than theirs" was not an idle saying. Raiders from the Head Splitters liked to carry off girls and young women whenever possible. Women of the People were traditionally tall, long-legged, and willowy in build, with facial features of outstanding beauty. ―

So it was no surprise that a young enemy chief would be attracted to the beautiful warrior woman. Both fugitives accepted this as a strong factor in the situation.

Both were still puzzled over the enemies' apparent wish to spare the life of Long Walker. It made no sense, especially if the young chief had developed a special attraction for Running Eagle. But then, who knows what Head Splitters think?

Long Walker was irritated and concerned that his companion had used the term "handsome" in speaking of the man. In truth, Running Eagle would have given much to recall those words the instant they were spoken. She had no idea why she had described the enemy chief in such terms. She only saw that she had hurt Walker deeply, and she was sorry. But to speak further of it would worsen the hurt.

At last it was fully dark. The drizzling rain had stopped, and only the occasional drip of water from the trees in the draw broke the silence.

Long Walker had prepared fire sticks and now knelt to kindle the blaze. It would be necessary to leave quickly after the fire was lighted. Even a small blaze would reflect a glow in the night. A few strokes of the fire bow produced a wisp of smoke, a few more a charred powder that spilled from the point of the whirling spindle. At last a glowing spark could be seen in the darkness.

Carefully Long Walker enfolded the spark in a handful of dry cedar bark he had sheltered from the rain. Holding it above his lips, he breathed life into the fire until it burst into flame. He thrust the tiny blaze into a prepared pocket beneath the pack rat's nest. Flames began to lick upward, hungrily surrounding the dry twigs.

Long Walker stepped back quickly, stripping the thong from his fire bow as he rose. It would be saved for later use, but the sticks were abandoned as too bulky to carry.

He followed Running Eagle along a dim game trail down the floor of the canyon, partially feeling his way until his eyes adjusted to the darkness. The girl led the way around a rocky ledge and into the brushy draw that concealed the horses.

They made their way quietly among the scrubby trees to the place where the horses were tethered, their muzzles tied. No, not here, Long Walker indicated, that next clump of trees. The two stepped forward, but the area looked entirely different in the darkness. It would be very easy to become disoriented.

For a moment a near panic gripped Running Eagle. Then she steadied herself. Never had a night looked blacker.

"We must stay together, Walker."

The two moved cautiously through the thicket, searching. Perhaps the animals had pulled free and wandered off.

They attempted to identify landmarks, unique shapes of rock or trees, but everything was different in the dark. Distances were deceptive, direction confused.

After searching for some time they encountered a stunted oak with a triple fork that both remembered.

"Walker, this is where we tied the horses!"

"Yes," he agreed sadly. "They are gone. We must move without them."

29

» » »

Black Fox was furious. His plan had been going so well. The head of the column, led by the two he wished to capture, passed through the narrow part of the trail. His warriors struck at the right moment from their hidden positions in the tall grass. The opposing war party had been effectively cut in two.

Crazy Woman and her companion were isolated with a handful of their warriors, and Black Fox's hidden bowmen swiftly cut the warriors down. He was elated when the bay stallion went down, further fragmenting the party of the warrior woman.

Then things began to turn wrong. The girl whirled her horse and returned to help the fallen warrior. Black Fox would never understand how the two had reached the shelter of the woods, riding double on her raw-boned gelding.

The time lost in hesitation before his charge into the trees had permitted the fugitives to escape. The dead warrior's body was discovered, and Black Fox's anger grew. He realized then that both the fugitives were well mounted.

There was more delay as the trackers painstakingly searched the opposite bank. Finally the signal came. The spot where the riders had quit the water was located. The pursuing party dashed across and spread out to search. It was not without great caution that the effort proceeded. Even outnumbered, the fugitives were the most dangerous warriors that the Head Splitters had faced.

The trail led into a rough and broken area, a canyon with many smaller spur canyons and small draws. There the trail disappeared. Black Fox fumed in rage, and the party split into ones and twos to comb the area.

There was a great deal of hesitation on the part of the younger warriors when it came to entering the dark gloom of the tree-shaded draws. Somewhere in the shadows crouched Crazy Woman and the tall man, waiting to strike from hiding. The knowledge that these two had sent many of their fellow tribesmen to the spirit world made the hairs rise on the necks of the searchers.

Consequently most of the search was carried out from the flat top of the ridge. The horsemen were riding along each fingerlike projection of land, looking down into the gullies between.

At one point there was a flurry of excitement. Two horses ran from a growth of dense brush and timber into a more open part of the canyon, frightened and with broken reins trailing. One of the animals was a nondescript brown mare, but the other created more interest. It was the unique white-splashed dun gelding of Crazy Woman.

Black Fox was jubilant. Now the fugitives were on foot. His warriors cautiously moved into the gully, looking into every bush and corner. Near the closed end of the draw, a rocky area seemed to partially conceal the entrance to a small opening or cleft, a cave in the limestone rock of the wall.

The searchers agreed that this must be the last hiding place of the two fugitives. Quietly they moved forward. Black Fox signaled, and dry wood was brought for a fire. They would smoke their quarry from hiding.

The fire was never lighted, however. From the depths of the dark cleft came a resentful, snarling growl. The warriors scattered, eager to be out of range of an irritable black bear, who now peered from the opening.

Immediately Black Fox reconstructed the situation. The fugitives had tied their horses and gone to hide elsewhere. The animals had scented the bear's den in the shifting breeze and had broken loose in panic.

Now, while he and his warriors followed a false trail, the girl and her companion were undoubtedly escaping. Angrily he motioned the men away from the bear's den. They must hurry now, because darkness was falling.

A light cloud bank moved across the sky, and drizzling rain began to fall. Almost frantically, Black Fox sent riders in all directions, looking for sign. All traces would be wiped out by the rain, if not found before dark.

The search was fruitless. One by one, riders returned to the camp fires along the canyon as darkness deepened. None had any findings to report. Black Fox paced angrily back and forth. Had Crazy Woman beaten him?

The strange mixture of hate and physical desire had now begun to dominate all his moves. He would find the woman. He must, or he would never rest.

Now he stood, hands on hips, staring at the black emptiness of the night. He scarcely felt the chill of the drizzling rain, so deep was his anger.

Then his eyes focused on a dim light in the distance, like the glow of the rising moon. But it could not be. The clouds and rain would cover the moon's face.

A fire! The answer finally occurred to him. The glow was firelight from a hidden blaze, reflected on the fog and haze of the low-hanging clouds.

A trick, of course. The fugitives would never light a

camp fire in such a situation. But it must be investigated, and that was probably their purpose. Black Fox called to a couple of men to follow him and moved off into the night.

They must move with caution. Their quarry was dangerous, and there was the gnawing doubt about the danger of death in the dark. It was possible, even, that Crazy Woman might have set this fire to draw the pursuers into ambush.

Black Fox moved forward, as quietly as possible, avoiding places which might conceal a hidden warrior. The others spread out on either side, slipping through the damp, waist-high grass, feeling their way in the dark. Ahead was the glow of the fugitives' fire. Even so, much time had passed before Black Fox could advance to a position affording a clear view of the fire.

There was no one there. Just as he had expected, Black Fox told himself. But it did not make him feel better about it.

Now he began to feel concern. If they were not by the fire, the two he sought were somewhere in the darkness, perhaps behind him. A cold chill crept between his shoulders and prickled along the back of his neck.

It was not worth the risk, he decided. The fugitives could not travel far in the dark. Softly he called to his companions, and they began a careful retreat. There should be no great difficulty in finding their quarry in the morning. After all, Crazy Woman and her companion were now known to be on foot.

30

>> >> >>

The fugitives traveled far during the time of darkness. It had taken only a short while to realize that with their horses gone, they must move rapidly.

Their direction of flight was a decision that mattered little. They considered what would be expected of them and tried to do otherwise. The Head Splitters would expect, they reasoned, that they would either try to return to their own Elk-dog band or to reach the Northern band. So it seemed that both the northern and southern trails would be watched. They must retreat either to the east or the west

The westward choice would take them closer to the country of the Head Splitters. Therefore, that would seem the less likely course. They would move westward, hoping their pursuers would waste time in searching the other directions.

Both Running Eagle and Long Walker saw this as only a temporary delay at best. The enemy trackers would soon find the trail. It would require much skill to avoid capture.

One other possibility seemed to present itself. If they could strike a lone pursuer or two and obtain horses, it would increase their chances.

But for now they must move. Thin, dripping clouds still obscured the stars, so their direction was largely established from memory of the terrain. They felt their way, stumbling sometimes, up and out of the gully to higher ground. There they could travel more rapidly in the open grassland.

When the clouds began to part, to reveal points of light like distant camp fires in the blackness of the sky, they were far away. As the clearing continued, they paused to establish direction.

"There!" Running Eagle pointed. "The Seven Hunters!"

"And the Real-star," Long Walker chuckled wryly. "Someone has moved it!"

Quickly they adjusted their course to the now well-established position of the stars and moved on. Once they were fortunate enough to find a shallow stream with a gravelly bottom and waded for some distance.

They left its protection to hide their tracks among those of a grazing herd of buffalo. The surprised animals raised shaggy heads to stare and snort at the two quiet figures slipping among them.

As morning drew close, they began to look for a hidden place to spend the daylight hours. A dark mass of heavy timber loomed ahead, and, before gray dawn began to show, the two established themselves in a hidden thicket of dogwood under the massive spreading boughs of giant sycamores.

Exhausted, they cuddled together to share body warmth against the chill of the morning damp. They shared one small robe, which had been tied to Running Eagle's saddle before the ambush.

Somehow, as they began to be more comfortable in the mutual warmth of the embrace, their physical contact seemed to change in purpose. Sleepily, Running Eagle pressed more firmly against her companion, enjoying his closeness.

Long Walker, though partly asleep, certainly had no

objection to this turn of events. He returned the girl's embrace, pressing closer against her warmth. Both were breathing more heavily now, face to face, lips searching hungrily for each other.

Suddenly Running Eagle pushed away and sat up, staring at him in angry accusation. Walker was never certain whether it had been a dream or the awakening that had spoiled the moment.

"I have my vows, Walker," she snapped.

Never had the young man been so frustrated. He had been willing to take what pleasure he could from her companionship, to help her in her plan of vengeance. He had done so and had felt that he had in some measure been able to guard her from some of the dangers of the trail she had chosen.

Now, he felt, she was misinterpreting his wish for physical closeness. It had been her reaction to the embrace, no less than his, which had brought out the desire in them both. Besides, there was an urgency in the situation that affected their actions.

"Running Eagle," he said softly, "vows mean little to one who is dead."

For a moment her gaze softened, then she shook her head as if to clear it. "No!" she said firmly.

She rose to pace impatiently around the clearing, apparently preoccupied in thought. Once, Long Walker thought she was about to speak, but she turned on her heel to continue her restless wandering. He drew the robe around his shoulders and curled up to attempt more rest.

The day seemed long. Several times they thought they heard the sounds of searchers. A horse called in the distance. The fugitives waited, weapons ready, but no one came.

They alternated their periods of rest, one watching and listening while the other slept. Running Eagle actually slept little during her turn at resting. Her mind was in too much turmoil. It was late in the day when she finally spoke of that which troubled her.

"Walker," she began gently, "I am sorry about this morning."

He shrugged indifferently, still hurt by her rejection.

"I wish it could be different," the girl pleaded. "It is only that I cannot be both persons at once."

She waited, but he said nothing.

"For now, Walker, it is important that we escape. I must be the best warrior that I can."

Still no answer.

"Walker," she was pleading now, "you know how important it is. It would be very dangerous to break my vows now. It could prevent our escape."

He smiled then, a little sadly.

"I know," he agreed. "It is only that I have always wanted it to be so different." He gave a long sigh. "But, you are right. First, we must escape."

Long Walker rose. "Evening is close. I will go to the top of the ridge to see where we must go tonight."

He picked up his lance and began the climb. The hill was steep, and in addition he must be as quiet as possible. Twice he thought he heard a noise and paused to assure himself that there were only the sounds of the prairie.

The last few paces to the top were the most uncomfortable because there was no way that he could see ahead. Carefully he looked over the low, rocky ledge, and after a long pause he pulled himself up and over. He saw nothing out of the ordinary. He crouched to look and listen and remained in a guarded position to wait for a long moment, while he listened to the call of a night bird along the stream. *Kookooskoos*, the great hunting owl, called his name from the gathering darkness somewhere below.

Finally Long Walker stood erect and relaxed. He looked to the west, where Sun Boy had just gone to his lodge on the other side, leaving a red glow behind on the horizon.

There was a rustling movement behind him, and Long Walker whirled, too late to meet the rush of two burly warriors. He fought fiercely but was never able to bring a weapon into play.

In the space of a few heartbeats his arms were pinned and bound behind him. His captors jerked him roughly to his feet to face a group of approaching warriors.

In the gathering dusk Long Walker recognized their leader. They had met before. The other man smiled thinly and opened the conversation in the sign language of the plains.

"Ah, we meet again! I am Black Fox." He paused a moment, then continued. "You will tell me now. Where is the woman?"

31
>> >> >>

Running Eagle rested, waiting quietly for Long
Walker to return. Shadows grew longer and darker,
and the creatures of the night began to awake and
start their activities. It was a pleasant time, this scrap
of evening that hung for a soft warm moment between the day and the darkness. A bird called, another
answered. There was the soft musical voice of the
spring a few steps away, as it trickled from the rock
ledge to fill a slight hollow at the base of the wall.

A coyote yapped from a distant hill, and the hollow
cry of the great owl sounded nearer at hand. The
darkness gathered, and Running Eagle picked up their
few belongings to be ready when Walker returned.

At full dark she began to wonder. As her heart
ticked away the time, her concern grew. Finally she
had to concede that something was totally wrong.
Walker should have returned long ago.

Now she berated herself for paying little attention.
Had Long Walker attempted to call out for help, perhaps while she, preoccupied, had enjoyed the quiet of

the twilight? The guilt that she felt over this possibility was overwhelming.

And where was her companion now? Had the enemy located her position from the direction taken by Long Walker? Had they forced him to reveal her whereabouts?

Something akin to panic gripped the girl. Her instincts told her to run, to remove herself from this hiding place. She turned and plunged into the thicket.

She had taken only a few steps, however, before her reason made her pause. Suppose, for a moment, that Long Walker had *not* been killed or captured. He might be out there somewhere in the night, skillfully avoiding their pursuers. If so, he would expect her to be where she could be found. He might even depend on her to be there, if he should be pursued on his return. Then she could ambush his pursuer. Yes, she owed it to Long Walker to remain where he had last seen her.

She stepped back through the thicket, into the little clearing, dropping the assortment of weapons and the robe that she carried. With a sigh of resignation, she sank to a sitting position.

It was, she recalled, the spot where they had lain together earlier. Gently, almost reverently, she touched the grassy knoll with her fingertips. She smiled sadly to herself. If only—

Irritated with her preoccupation, she shook her head to clear it. She must force herself to think her way through this crisis. Wishing about what could not be would only interfere with her ability to function

She remembered something her uncle, Owl, had once said. "You look, but you do not see."

At the time he had been attempting to show her the nest of a green heron. They were crouched to peer between the stems of the rushes along a quiet pool.

"See, the bird stands in the reeds on the other side," he whispered.

The girl looked and looked but could see only the myriad of foliage, the slender stems and leaves reflected by the smooth surface. Frustrated, a little irri-

tated, she began to study each individual stem, one at
a time.

Then she saw the eye. Bright, unblinking, pale yellow in the sunlight, the bird's gaze was focused directly on her. In an instant the entire bird was clearly
visible. It remained completely motionless, but with
the new knowledge she now had, its form was quite
plain.

The eye, of course, was in one side of a slender
head. The elongated beak unmovingly pointed upward,
mimicking the pointed blades of the reeds. The entire
coloration of the heron, it could now be seen, was
intended to confuse the observer.

Narrow stripes of dark green, buff, and red-brown
alternated to produce the effect of the thicket of rushes.
Even standing completely in the open, the creature
could blend against the background of water plants
and be unseen to a casual observer. She had been
thrilled at the discovery.

"You look, but you do not see."

Was there that which was not easily seen about this
present situation? She leaned back against the tree
trunk to think again of the circumstances of her being
here in the darkness of the prairie night.

First, for reasons not entirely plain, their pursuers
wanted both her and Long Walker alive. In her own
case she had suspected that the enemy chieftain looked
on her with desire. As for their reasons for keeping
Walker alive, she was puzzled. It did seem that they
could have killed him easily, however, if they had
wished.

She set aside this puzzle to move on in her thinking. Why had Walker not returned? If he were able to,
he surely would have done so by this time. Even if he
were pursued, he could have managed to elude or
trick the enemy before this. Add to this theory the
known reluctance of the Head Splitters to engage in
night conflict. Yes, Walker would have managed to
return to her if he were able.

She accepted with reluctance the answer she sought.

He had not returned, so it must be that he was unable to do so. The only reasons she could think of were that he must be dead or captured.

Her mind recoiled from the first possibility, but she must look at it again. Once more she studied the fact that the enemy had earlier rejected the opportunity to kill Long Walker. Could the young enemy chief have thought of some use for Long Walker alive?

Suddenly the entire thing became clear in her mind, just as with the heron so long ago. She had been looking directly at it, but not seeing.

If the young Head Splitter wanted her, then he might use Long Walker to achieve his goal. The more she thought, the more certain it seemed. Somewhere beyond the ridge was the camp of the enemy war party, and in that camp Long Walker was almost surely a prisoner.

Yes, now everything seemed to fit. Once more Running Eagle realized her choices were narrowing.

She need no longer fear pursuit. The Head Splitters had no reason to try to capture her. Now she would come to them.

For a moment she thought of attempting to approach by stealth to free Long Walker. She quickly abandoned the thought. They would be on guard for such a move.

No, there was only one course open to her now to save Long Walker. She knew what she must do. She stretched on the robe to lie sleeplessly, waiting for morning.

When the gray of the false dawn began to brighten the east, she rose and gathered her weapons. She tossed the robe across her shoulder and began the ascent to the top of the ridge.

Boldly she swung over the last ledge and stood upright on the flat top of the hill. The first rays of the sun slanted across the prairie. The girl swept the surrounding landscape with her glance, searching. To the west hung a blue-gray haze of smoke from morning camp fires, and Running Eagle turned in that direction, along the ridge. She had traveled only a short distance when a warrior rose from a thin clump of sumac on the hillside, his bow ready.

The girl stopped, and, still standing erect, she raised her right hand, palm outward. The enemy warrior came cautiously forward, but she signaled him to stop.

"I would talk with your chief," she said in sign talk.

The man considered a moment, then nodded. "Come," he beckoned.

He set off at a swinging trot, and Running Eagle followed.

32
⟩⟩ ⟩⟩ ⟩⟩

Black Fox watched the approach of his scout, followed closely by the warrior woman, with a great deal of satisfaction.

It had been a great stroke of good fortune that the tall man, now known by name as Long Walker, had fallen into their hands. The war party, preparing to camp for the night, had happened to be near the point where he climbed from the ravine. They had quickly signaled each other to silence and concealed themselves to seize the fugitive when he pulled himself over the ledge.

Ah, how things sometimes go right! Black Fox gloated in the strength of his medicine as they made camp, and he began to question the prisoner. There were those who would have killed the man outright, and even more who wished to test his manhood by torture and mutilation. But Black Fox had a better plan. It depended on keeping the prisoner alive and in good condition.

He talked with the man, using the sign talk, and

learned that his name was Long Walker. The girl they spoke of as Crazy Woman was called Running Eagle by her people. Black Fox found it amusing that she did not bear "woman" as part of her name.

"Among the Head Splitters," he signaled proudly, "a warrior's name would not be worn by a woman."

"Among the Head Splitters," Long Walker retorted, "there is no warrior like Running Eagle!"

The man was infuriating in his insolence, but Black Fox could wait and play out his game. He attempted to determine more about the relationship between the man and the girl.

"Just friends," Long Walker replied with a shrug.

He used the hand sign for comrades or fellow warriors. Black Fox was not entirely convinced. There was some special relationship here, and on this his plan depended.

The two were so inseparable in all the tales and legends about them that there had to be a special meaning of some sort. If one were a prisoner, the other would attempt rescue.

With this in mind the camp was placed in an open area and heavily guarded. The prisoner was tied to a pole between two trees, in plain sight. He would be bait for the trap.

Actually Black Fox had little thought that the girl would make a rescue attempt. She would realize that the prisoner would be heavily guarded and could be killed at the first threat of attack. No, she would wait for daylight and then seek a parley.

And he had been right, so it seemed. One of the scouts who had been posted in the area of Long Walker's capture was escorting her into the camp.

A couple of young warriors sprang forward to seize her, but the girl stopped them with a hand sign and a withering glance.

"What hospitality is this?" she gestured indignantly. "I come to talk with your chief!"

Black Fox smiled to himself. Many men in such circumstances would have lost their nerve. This remarkable girl not only maintained her haughty composure, but she had just given his young men a lesson in the etiquette of visiting another's camp.

She strode forward boldly and marched straight to where Black Fox sat, his back against a small tree. Both were relaxed, weapons not at ready. There would be no surprise moves here, for the implied terms of this parley were those of a truce.

"I have come to bargain for your prisoner," the girl began.

She had barely glanced at Long Walker, except to assure herself that he was alive and well. She dared not look at the stricken expression on his face.

"How?" Black Fox's retort was not really a question. "You have nothing to offer."

"I will meet you in combat. If I win, we both go free. If you kill me, you do as you wish."

Black Fox laughed aloud. "Why should I fight you? I might be injured." He cowered in mock fear, then continued. "No, I wish to keep him. You should not challenge me, anyway. You should be in a lodge, in some man's bed, not trying to be a warrior."

He was teasing her, and he saw that her anger rose. For a moment he wondered if she were about to break the rules of etiquette and strike at him.

"Now, I might consider," he continued thoughtfully, "an exchange of the right kind. But you have nothing." He spread his hands in mock perplexity, enjoying this moment. "Unless, of course, you would exchange yourself for this prisoner."

"No!" shouted Long Walker, twisting at the thongs that bound his wrists to the pole. "No, Running Eagle! Do not do this!"

The girl turned, white-faced, to look at him for the first time during the parley. "It will be all right, Walker." She spoke in their own tongue, not familiar to their captors. Her voice was a trifle tense, but confident. "I will escape later."

Black Fox interrupted. "Stop! There will be no talking to my prisoner!" he warned.

A torrent of protest poured forth from Long Walker until Black Fox stepped over and inserted a rawhide thong between his teeth, tying it cruelly tight behind his neck. Walker's yelling subsided to a murmur of ineffectual sound.

"What arrangements?" the girl was asking.

"None. He goes free, I keep you."

"No." She spoke firmly. "He must have a horse and weapons."

Black Fox shook his head. The woman was driving a hard bargain.

"A horse, no weapons," he insisted.

"He is not to be tied, and not followed when he leaves here?"

"Agreed. But if he tries to return he will be killed."

The girl nodded. "Of course."

She stepped over to the prisoner and confidently cut his bonds. "Do not worry, Walker. I will escape when I can," she whispered.

Long Walker's frustration was evident. Had it not been for the rules of the truce he would have attacked Black Fox in an instant. "I will come for you, Running Eagle," he promised. "Watch for me."

A young warrior stepped forward and struck Walker across the shoulders with a quirt, hoping to goad him into an unwise move. Walker gave the youngster only a glance, then stepped over to face Black Fox.

"You think this is a great day, Head Splitter. Your troubles have only started. You will not live long enough to forget, and we will see the vultures pick your bones."

Only a momentary expression of doubt crossed the face of Black Fox, then he smiled. "Bring a horse for this man," he chuckled. Then an amusing twist occurred to him. "Let it be the horse of Crazy Woman!" he called.

A man led the white-splotched dun forward, with only a simple thong looped around the lower jaw as a war bridle. There was no saddle or pad, but Long Walker easily vaulted to the animal's back.

"Take him well away from the camp," instructed Black Fox to two mounted warriors near by.

"And kill him?"

"No! Not unless he tries to return. He is under the truce."

Long Walker turned to look over his shoulder once more. "Remember! I will be back for you!" he called.

"No, Walker! They will kill you. I will escape!"

She watched until the three riders disappeared over the crest of the hill. At least she had been successful in freeing Long Walker. She turned to face her captor and laid her weapons at his feet.

"There must be no treachery," she cautioned. "If Long Walker is harmed, I will know. Then there is no way you will escape me."

"Escape?" Black Fox snorted. "You are the one who will never escape." He stepped forward and looped a thong around each of her wrists.

"Over here," he motioned. He knotted the fetters on her wrists to the overhead pole, so recently the place of Long Walker's imprisonment.

"You will remain tied," Black Fox informed her in sign talk, "until we reach our village. Then the other women in my lodge will show you your duties."

He turned on his heel and strode away to prepare to depart.

33

>> >> >>

Long Walker, flanked by the two Head Splitters, rode slowly out of the enemy camp. He had never been so furious, so frustrated, so utterly helpless. He raged inwardly.

Only one thought prevented him from attacking the warriors who rode beside him. Common sense told him that they would kill him immediately at the slightest cue. Then there would be no one at all to attempt the rescue of Running Eagle.

At the very thought of the girl, carried away as a prisoner to the lodge of Black Fox, he could have screamed out in grief and frustration. But it would do no good and might provoke these warriors into action.

So Long Walker sat upright on his horse, looking straight ahead. He did not know how far these men would escort him. He was not concerned about the possibility of treachery. Custom was too strong. These men had merely been assigned to make certain that the erstwhile prisoner actually left the area.

They were pointing his course due south, back

toward his own band. So be it. He would let it appear that he followed that trail.

One of the warriors now motioned him to stop. Long Walker tensed, ready for any surprise move.

"You go," the young warrior motioned. "If you try to return we will kill you!"

Walker was greatly tempted to make a statement as to the relative likelihood of longevity for himself and for Black Fox. He decided against such an inflammatory remark, saving it for a better moment.

Suddenly Owl Dung leaped forward, nearly unseating his rider. Long Walker looked back, catching only a flying glimpse of what had precipitated the plunge. The other of the enemy warriors, who had ridden in sullen silence until this point, was laughing uproariously. He had struck the horse across the rump with a quirt to make it bolt, hoping to unseat the rider.

Long Walker realized that this was the same man who had struck him across the back earlier. This would be the sort of man who enjoyed the torture of prisoners. Walker marked him well for future reference. The time might come when he would wish to remember.

He cantered away, trying to appear dejected and beaten, suppressing the impulse to toss a final obscene gesture at the two laughing enemy warriors. They must think him completely defeated.

Once out of sight, he waited to make certain he was not followed and then turned due west. As he rode, his mind was working rapidly.

The Head Splitters would immediately start for their own people, somewhere to the west or southwest. He must follow without being detected and be aware of the exact location of Running Eagle's imprisonment Then he would plan the moment and the manner of her rescue.

But first he must have food and weapons. Especially weapons. With a bow or a lance he could obtain food. A knife, also, might be helpful.

The most obvious course of action was to strike an

enemy sentry in the dark and take his weapons. Long Walker soon rejected this plan. Aside from the risk it involved to himself, there was Running Eagle to think of. It would not be unlikely for the frustrated Head Splitters to take vengeance on the prisoner. No, he must avoid all contact with the Head Splitters, *any* Head Splitters, until his plan was complete. He must find another way.

He traveled rapidly, and by late afternoon he felt that he was well ahead of the enemy war party. Somewhere in the area, he knew, was a village of Growers. They would furnish him with food and a place to spend the night. The open prairie could be quite cold at this time of year, especially without so much as a robe for protection.

It was nearly dark before he located the Growers' village. He did so by following the most prominent of the streams he could find. Not until he was riding in did an idea occur to him that might be fruitful.

Followed by yapping dogs and staring children, Long Walker walked his horse among the log and dirt dwellings until he found a prosperous-looking one that looked familiar. He dismounted and called out politely at the door. A woman thrust her head out, then quickly withdrew it.

In a few moments she came outside, followed by a suspicious man, probably her husband. The approach of a lone stranger, poorly equipped and unarmed, was a situation that required caution.

Long Walker opened the parley quickly in the gathering twilight. He knew only a few words of the Growers' tongue, but the sign talk was universal.

"I am Long Walker, of the Elk-dog People, the band of Heads Off."

"Yes," answered the woman. "I remember you now. Your band traded with us last season."

Both Growers relaxed somewhat. Nearly every year they had some contact with the tribe of this man, trading their corn, beans, and pumpkins for the meat and skins of the hunters.

Long Walker knew that they must remain perfectly impartial in a situation such as his own crisis. Still, there were ways to use their help.

"I have been a prisoner of a Head Splitter war party," he explained. "I have no weapons, only this horse."

The two nodded understandingly.

"You wish to trade the horse?" the man inquired.

"No, I need the horse. I come to hunt, for you."

Rapidly he outlined his plan. If someone would loan him a bow or a lance, he would try for a buffalo kill near the Growers' village. Then all the meat and the skin would be theirs, in exchange for weapons and a few supplies.

The couple conferred for a few moments in their own tongue, expressions of doubt plain on their faces. The husband stepped to a nearby lodge and called something to the occupants. Another man joined him, and a third. There was much animated conversation. Finally the man to whom Long Walker had first spoken returned.

"Blackbird will let you use his bow." He indicated one of the other men. "If you are successful in the hunt, we will trade. If not, you return his bow."

Long Walker nodded. "Will someone let me use a robe for tonight?"

A woman handed him a ragged buffalo robe. He accepted it gratefully, only hoping for a moment that its previous occupant was not infested by many lice. He curled against the outside wall of one of the lodges and fell asleep almost instantly. It had been long since he had slept without the threat of death or capture. He could eat later.

By the time daylight allowed him to see for the hunt, Long Walker was searching for buffalo. A few of the men in the village had expressed resentment and scorn at the suggestion that the stranger could best them at hunting. Most, however, realized that a man of one of the hunter tribes would be more skilled than one of the Growers. That was the way of things.

Walker was pleased to note that there were several small bands of buffalo in the immediate area. One group was grazing slowly in the direction of the village. He wondered if it might not be possible to help the Growers make a larger kill. He could see that at one point the valley narrowed. A few men could conceal themselves and perhaps kill several of the animals. He rode along the ridge and attempted to plan the best strategy for the hunt.

Then, from the advantage of his new position, he saw an alarming development. Approaching from the east was a column of riders. They were some distance away, but there was little doubt as to their identity. It could be no other than the war party he had just left.

There was a moment of panic, then reason returned. The war party could not be searching for him. They would have no reason to do so. The Head Splitters were merely traveling, returning to their own people, while Long Walker was, in effect, doing the same. Since their destination was the same, their paths would easily cross. He must remember this and be more careful.

For the present, quick action was necessary. The village of the Growers was, in a way, a haven of refuge. It would be against the code of conduct to attack an enemy in the village of neutral friends and traders.

Still, Long Walker wished to avoid all contact with the Head Splitters if possible. There would be questions, doubts, and embarrassment for the Growers. The impression he wished to leave was that of a man beaten, fleeing for his life. At the same time, he must have weapons.

Reluctantly he rejected the thought of staying close enough to catch a glimpse of Running Eagle. There would be time for that later.

He headed straight for the village of the Growers, looking all the while for the buffalo that he sought. A fat young cow raised her head to stare at him curiously as he approached. Long Walker fitted an arrow to the bowstring.

Owl Dung sensed the pursuit and sprinted forward as the cow whirled to run. Long Walker's arrow struck the selected spot, and the animal stumbled and fell to lie kicking in the grass.

Now, scarcely pausing to look at the dying buffalo, he urged the horse on toward the village. He slid to a stop before the lodges.

"Blackbird!" he called loudly.

The man emerged from the doorway.

"Your buffalo is there," he pointed. "I must go. There are Head Splitters coming. I keep your bow."

Without waiting for an answer, he urged the horse into a fast canter away from the village.

He was pleased with the manner in which things had happened. The closemouthed Growers, if they mentioned him at all, would describe him as a frightened fugitive, running for his life. This was the impression he meant to leave for the enemy war party.

More important, his contact with the Growers had suggested the beginning of a plan for the rescue of Running Eagle.

34

>> >> >>

Since arriving back at his people's summer camp,
Black Fox had experienced continual frustration.

There had been the celebration of the defeat and
capture of the enemy warrior woman, which was grat-
ifying, of course. Dances, songs, and ceremonies honoring the deeds of the successful war party had lasted
for several days. The captive Running Eagle had been
displayed for all to see, to marvel at her beauty, and to
wonder that such a woman could be a ruthless warrior. Many men envied Black Fox, in whose lodge she
would remain.

Black Fox accepted the envy as graciously as was
required, as he had the honors of the dance and celebration. Privately he was more frustrated than ever.

When he had only thought and dreamed of the girl,
distant and unattainable, the stress was bad enough.
Now it was even worse, an eventuality that had not
occurred to him.

The girl submitted to his demands, it was true, but
the manner in which she did so was a denial. Her

haughty pride, her aloofness, were untouchable. Try as he might, Black Fox could not shake the feeling of loathing that he saw in her eyes. It was as if she looked at some repulsive, unwholesome creature. To make matters worse, it made him feel inferior, degraded somehow.

Then, in resentment and anger at this feeling, he would approach her again, only to experience an even stronger repulsion. Mixed with all this was the defiance in her glance. It was like that of a fettered eagle, captured but never tamed, defiant until the end of life itself.

To Black Fox this proud demeanor only increased her desirability, and hence his frustration. He smiled outwardly at the ribald remarks of his friends who envied him the possession of the girl. Inwardly he became more and more depressed.

He wished sometimes that he could be rid of her. She could be sold, of course. Any one of a number of influential men in the tribe would pay him many horses and robes for her. Their leering, sidelong glances at her told that plainly. Unfortunately such a transaction would reveal the truth to all—that possession of this girl was not the triumph that it seemed.

Sometimes he even wished that he had killed her initially. That would have avoided his present problems. Now it was too late. To kill her now would also be an admission of the disappointment that he found in her.

To some extent he began to avoid her. That was better than her flat, emotionless submission, while her eyes blazed with the degrading mixture of pride and loathing for him.

He no longer knew exactly what he wanted from her. He was no longer certain that her spirit could be broken. There had never been a woman like this, at least not in the experience of Black Fox. If, indeed, he could overcome her pride and force her to accept the situation as he saw it, would it only make matters worse? Would her dull, colorless acceptance become more of a problem than he found it now?

Black Fox was not accustomed to such response, or lack of response, from women. Yes, that must be what was missing in the relationship. Above all, what he wanted was not mere possession of the girl. It was for *her* to come to *him*. If the beautiful dark eyes would only show the fire of desire instead of the burning coals of hatred.

But how was he to achieve this? He had treated her well. After the initial period of her captivity he had not even tied her. How could she ask for better treatment? He had spared the life of her warrior consort, Long Walker, when he could have killed him.

Ah, that one! Black Fox pondered often that Running Eagle had undoubtedly approached Long Walker with the fire in her eyes that he wished for himself. He should have killed the man!

But it had worked well. Long Walker had been shamed, his freedom traded for that of a woman. He had retreated, tail between his legs. Even the chance near meeting at the village of the Growers had been ludicrous. Long Walker had apparently made a buffalo kill nearby but had been forced to abandon it at the approach of the war party. He had slunk away, as a coyote abandons a buffalo carcass at the approach of wolves.

Still, it rankled Black Fox that the man had something that he desired—the affection of Running Eagle. He sat against his willow backrest and watched her at her work. It was frustrating to watch the graceful curves of her body, her supple, willowy motions. It aroused him, then embittered him as he was reminded once more that the taste of victory had turned to ashes in his mouth. Yet he could not refrain from looking.

She was dressing skins beside the lodge. The other wives of Black Fox worked a little apart from Running Eagle. Their dislike for the beautiful captive was apparent. Black Fox supposed it was because of jealousy.

No matter. They could adjust. If only he could, he reflected miserably.

An old woman hobbled down the path among the lodges, leaning on a stick. A basket of corn was balanced on her other hip. She was apparently from the nearby Grower village, offering corn to trade. She was bundled in a tattered robe which she had pulled around her ears against the chill of the wind.

The old ones feel the wind's chill more sharply, Black Fox observed to himself. The weather was really quite pleasant.

The Grower woman paused to barter in the sign talk with a wife at a neighboring lodge. She handed a few ears of corn and tucked the cylinder of pemmican she received in exchange into her basket. Then she approached the spot where Running Eagle worked.

"Not her," Black Fox called. "The other women!"

The old Grower apparently did not understand. She turned, confused, and her foot struck some small obstruction in the path. The woman pitched headlong on her face, spilling her basket's contents on the ground.

Painfully she rose to her knees, retrieved the basket, and began to pick up the scattered ears of corn. Running Eagle stepped over to help her.

Black Fox was amused. Seldom did the Growers actively enter the camp of the hunting tribes to trade. Usually the hunters, more mobile by habit, approached the Growers.

Somewhere in the back of his mind a warning buzzed, like the rattle of a real-snake. He half rose for a better look at the old woman. Her back was toward him, and a bare leg protruded from beneath the tattered robe. It was not the wizened limb of an old woman, but the muscular, bronzed leg of a warrior.

"Stop!" Black Fox yelled.

The Grower sprang erect and threw the robe aside, turning to face the astonished Black Fox. From the mouth of the newcomer now came the unmistakable, deep-throated war cry of the People.

Long Walker sprang forward, swinging the walking

stick as a weapon. Black Fox jumped aside, seized a war club, and parried the next blow. Men came running.

"I want him alive!" shouted Black Fox.

The first man went down under his staff's blow, but the wave of numbers overwhelmed Long Walker. In a few moments he was seized, disarmed, tied, and dragged before Black Fox.

"So!" Black Fox chuckled. "We meet again!"

35
» » »

Long Walker found himself trussed tightly and shoved roughly forward. He was wild with despair. His plan had failed.

It had seemed good, the scheme to enter the Head Splitter camp disguised as a Grower. No one would pay him any attention, and he would not be expected to know the tongue of the Head Splitters. He could communicate in sign talk and move freely about the camp to locate Running Eagle's place of imprisonment.

He had taken time to plan the move in detail, complete with the garments of an old woman, her basket, and her corn. The Growers drove a hard bargain. He had only the horse and the bow he had obtained from Blackbird to use in trading. The Growers knew this well.

This village was conveniently located only a short distance from the camp of the Head Splitters. The hunter tribes often camped in such proximity to facilitate trading and gathering of winter supplies.

So, Long Walker reasoned, it would not be unusual

for a Grower woman to enter the camp of his enemies. It would be overlooked as a common occurrence.

And it had almost been successful. He had found Running Eagle and had contrived to spill the basket of corn almost at her feet. He had hoped to be able to hand her a small knife which he had obtained in trade from the Growers.

He knew that, as a prisoner, the girl would not be allowed to have any weapons at hand. If her chores required the use of a knife, or even a flint awl or scraper, it would be taken from her at the completion of the task. She would be regarded as a dangerous prisoner.

He had taken the sharp flint from the folds of his tattered robe and was actually in the act of handing it to her when Black Fox shouted. *Aiee*, then things happened so rapidly.

Knowing that he was discovered, Long Walker rose to fight. He was able to land but a single blow before he was overwhelmed, tied tightly, and dragged before the gloating Black Fox. His second knife, more suited for fighting, had been stripped from him. In the confused melee he had no idea what had happened to the knife he had attempted to give to the girl.

Now worse had come to worst. He would be tortured and killed, no doubt, probably before the eyes of Running Eagle. Well, so be it. He would show them the pride with which a man of the People could die.

Running Eagle was dragged up beside him, also bound tightly. His heart sank as he saw the despair in her eyes.

"I am sorry, Running Eagle. I have failed you."

"No, no, Walker. It could not be helped."

Black Fox stepped forward and struck Long Walker across the face with his quirt. "Silence, dog!"

He spoke in his own tongue, then remembered that the prisoner would not understand and repeated in sign talk. Black Fox was enjoying this scene.

Long Walker was thinking rapidly. Perhaps the pride of the Head Splitter could be utilized. He motioned with his head toward his bound wrists, indicating the wish to talk.

After a long pause Black Fox nodded, chuckling with amusement. He cut the thongs, and Walker rubbed his wrists a moment to restore circulation. Then he began to sign, carefully, plainly, and boldly.

"Your mother eats dung, Head Splitter. Are you afraid to fight men, and only make war on women? I spit in your face!"

He proceeded to do so. Black Fox started to react, then steadied, suspecting trickery.

"Are you afraid to fight me?" Walker persisted.

"No, Walker, please," Running Eagle pleaded.

He waved her to silence.

"No, let her talk, too," chuckled Black Fox.

He reached forward and cut her bonds, also. Now he was thoroughly enjoying the prisoners' plight. Long Walker pressed on.

"Are you afraid to fight me, Head Splitter? You have never faced me without my hands tied!"

Black Fox glowered, then resumed his chuckle.

"Fight me for her," Walker persisted.

Running Eagle crowded forward, using hand signs rapidly. "No! Fight me! If I win, Long Walker goes free!"

"Are you afraid, Black Fox? Either of us will meet you in combat."

Black Fox appeared to hesitate a moment, then shook his head decisively. He laughed, long and loud.

"Why should I fight either of you? I have you both as prisoners. You cannot ask such a privilege!"

The circle of Head Splitters, who had gathered to satisfy their curiosity over the excitement, roared with laughter.

"Now, what shall I do with you?" Black Fox seemed to ponder, and the onlookers chuckled with delight. "We will talk no more of fighting. I will say what is to be."

Now his manner changed, and his face hardened. "You will both be kept alive," he began. Then he turned to Running Eagle. "Long Walker will be treated well only as long as you do as I wish. If I become unhappy with you, his torture starts."

He paused, and his look and gestures left no doubt as to the sort of torture that was intended. The circle was quiet now. The onlookers seemed to realize that the time for laughter was gone, for now Black Fox was deadly serious.

Long Walker's heart sank. There was nothing more he could do. Now he had failed completely. Not only had his rescue plan been unsuccessful, but he had been unable to goad their captor into unwise combat.

Black Fox was right, of course. There was no reason for him to engage in conflict with either of the prisoners. They were already totally in his power.

A final, unpleasant thought struck Long Walker. Now he had not only failed, but he had provided the enemy the best of weapons. Until now, Running Eagle had been able to be defiant, to protest, to cause trouble, and in any conceivable way to show her loathing for the Head Splitters.

With the capture of Long Walker, she could now be controlled. He knew that she would allow no harm to come to him, and she would do whatever she must to protect him. It was a clever insight on the part of Black Fox.

As he realized the hopelessness of the situation, Walker also realized that without him there would be no such control over the girl. If he were killed, she would be free to act as she wished.

Without hesitation he launched himself directly at the nearest warrior, seized the man's war club, and turned to strike at Black Fox.

The young chief had correctly anticipated this move. As Long Walker turned, the heavy handle of Black Fox's war club thumped loudly across the side of his head. Black Fox looked quickly at Running Eagle to forestall any move on her part, but she was staring at the limp form of Long Walker.

"Tie them both," he muttered to a warrior at his

elbow, "but handle the man gently. I want him in good condition."

He pointed to a pole beside his lodge. "Tie the man there."

He turned to Running Eagle and pointed in sign talk. "You! Inside the lodge."

36
>> >> >>

Black Fox lay on his bed in the darkness, waiting for the girl to come to him. He could hardly contain his delight. At last he had found a way to control the beautiful warrior woman of the enemy. The mere thought of the power over her that he now possessed made him smile in the darkness.

She had slumped for a time in sullen submission after his ultimatum. He watched her, in the dimness of the lodge, as she glanced at him from time to time. He smoked his pipe and waited.

Finally the girl tossed her head and motioned toward her bound hands. She was still sullen, anger plain on her face, but she wished to talk. Black Fox freed her from the thongs and stood waiting while she rubbed her chafed wrists. When he could stand it no longer, he opened the conversation with an inquiry.

"You wish to talk with me?"

She glared a moment, then her face softened. She answered the question with a question. "What do you wish me to do?"

Black Fox studied the girl's face a long time. Yes, it might be, he decided. For the very first time since he had known her, she now seemed ready and willing to cooperate.

He had finally discovered the means to control the spirited warrior. The threat of harm to her companion had accomplished what force or threats to herself could not. She appeared willing to do anything to protect Long Walker.

The cunning Black Fox recognized the power of the medicine he now possessed. He must think this through, slowly and carefully, to use this unexpected turn of events to his best advantage.

"What do you wish?" she signaled again.

Plan carefully, he reminded himself. First, make certain that she knows her warrior is treated well.

He spoke to one of the other women and rose to step outside, beckoning Running Eagle to follow. There, while the girl watched, Black Fox retied the prisoner's bonds in a more comfortable manner. He beckoned to the woman who had followed them, and she gave Long Walker a drink from a water skin. Then she sat down before him and began to feed him.

"He must remain tied, because I do not trust him," Black Fox explained, "but you can see that he is being treated well."

The girl nodded, appearing perplexed.

"This treatment will continue, if your actions are good. If not . . ."

He paused and fondled his knife suggestively. Running Eagle was still puzzled.

"Yes, you have said this. What must I do that I have not?"

Black Fox hoped to make his meaning plain. "You have forced me to come to you, and you have rejected me. I am a chief of my people. You should be proud to share my lodge. *That* is what you must do."

"I do not understand."

"You must show pride and pleasure in being with me. *You* must come to *me*, now."

The prisoner called out to her, a torrent of protest which Black Fox did not understand. There was no question, however, as to the meaning of the girl's answer. She dismissed the other with a casual wave of her hand and looked back to Black Fox. There was a look of understanding in her eyes, and now the beginning of a smile.

It was a smile, in fact, coupled with a sultry glance through half-lowered lashes. The entire look was so suggestive, so provocative, that he was certain now that she not only understood his meaning, but had accepted it.

"Of course, my chief."

Somehow her answer was seductive, even in sign talk. Then she held a hand before her in caution, palm outward, before resuming. "But you must give me a little time."

Black Fox nodded mechanically and ran his tongue over his suddenly dry lips. This was progressing far better than he could have imagined.

The girl continued, again with a smile that held hidden promises. "I will come to you, after darkness has come."

For the rest of the daylight time, Black Fox watched her, trying all the while to pretend not to do so. When their glances happened to meet from time to time, there was always the flash of secret promise in her eyes. Several times he caught her sidelong glance under long dark lashes. Ah, that he should be so fortunate! He could hardly wait until the time of darkness.

Running Eagle, now freed for the day from the chores of the lodge, busied herself with other things. Under the resentful watch of the other women, she bathed in the stream. She washed, dried, and smoothed her long hair, finally braiding it after the fashion of the People. If the Head Splitters had known, they might have observed that her braids were those of a woman, not in the style of a man who takes the war path.

Her garment was a woman's dress of the captor's tribe. Black Fox had insisted that she wear it since her capture. She had cleansed the dress as well as she was able and dried it in the warm autumn sunlight. Now she dressed herself and returned to the lodge of Black Fox.

She sat next to him during the evening meal, choosing special morsels of food to place in his mouth with her fingers. The two other women of the lodge were furious at her bold advances, but Black Fox angrily waved them away and returned to lighthearted dalliance with Running Eagle.

"You will see to your own duties. We wish to be alone," he called after them.

When the sun had slid below earth's rim, Running Eagle excused herself. "I will go and prepare for the night," she told him in sign talk. "I will come to you soon." She gently touched his chest in a gesture of promise and stepped outside.

As he waited impatiently on his pallet of robes, Black Fox again wondered at his good fortune and the strength of his medicine. Soon the girl would come to him, in all the strength and beauty she had promised.

And yes, *she* must come to *him*. He intended to abide by that demand. He would not approach her. She must be the one to take the initiative.

Then the flap of the doorway lifted, and he saw her graceful figure in dim outline against the shadowy darkness outside. There was no fire in the lodge, and the blackness as the door skin dropped back into place was complete.

The other two women had retired, and soft snores came from one of the beds. There was no sound from the other. Little Bird had been the more jealous and would be lying awake in anger. It was no matter, Black Fox knew. Wives often resented the intrusion of a new woman. She would get over it

Running Eagle came now to his bed, dropping to her knees beside him. She was breathing heavily as she leaned over him. Her hands caressed the bare skin of his chest and shoulders. He felt her shift her weight, and the warmth of her firm body pressed against his

Ah, this was more like it, Black Fox exulted to himself. Her face was next to his, her breath still panting heavily in his ear in the darkness. Her fingers wandered across his shoulders and his throat, and she caressed his ears, making the hairs stand on his neck.

She scratched playfully beneath the angle of his jaw, murmuring soft little phrases in her own tongue. He did not understand the words, but from the tone of her whisper he assumed this to be part of the passionate ritual of love among her people. Luxuriously he stretched his chin upward to expose his throat to her caressing touch. Then came a moment when a doubt entered his mind. He was partially pinned down beneath the delicious burden of her body. The girl was scratching at his throat, and he was exposing it for her. This was not a thing of good judgment in the presence of a potential enemy.

Suppose, his mind wandered in sudden alarm, suppose the man, Long Walker, had managed to hand her a small knife or other easily concealed instrument. The time when he fell and spilled the corn! Their hands had been busy, together, for only one instant, but there had been no one to see! If he had given her a knife, then this would be the time she would choose—

There was little pain as the sharp flint sliced across his throat. He struggled to rise as he felt the warm trickle of his own blood on his neck. The girl sat astride his body now, knees pinning his arms while a hand over his mouth kept him from crying out. Panic gripped him, and he tried to escape her hold. But she was incredibly strong, and he felt himself weakening rapidly. His last thought as he slipped into unconsciousness was of the time of darkness, when a spirit may not find its way to the other side.

As the struggles of Black Fox ceased, Running Eagle continued her rhythmic panting, accompanied by low exclamations, as if in the heat of passion. She was certain that Little Bird was awake, and the sounds of this death struggle must appear to be those of ecstasy.

Finally she lay quietly for a time, cooling and resting after her exertions. Then she gave a deep sigh and rose, making no pretense at quiet. This was a critical moment. It must appear a natural and logical thing to go outside.

She sighed again and picked up her discarded dress from the floor near Black Fox's bed. She slipped through the door skin and let it fall. The buckskin dress fell quickly over her head and into place. Once more she gave a long, contented sigh for the benefit of any listening ears, then stepped quickly to the place where Long Walker was tied.

"Walker!" she whispered in his ear. "It is time." Deftly, she cut the bonds on his wrists and ankles. "Come."

She took his hand to lead the way among the lodges to the meadow where the horse herd grazed.

37
>> >> >>

It would have been quicker to steal a horse or two from their places near the lodges. Each warrior kept one of his best animals ready for emergencies tied next to his dwelling.

But to loose these horses and lead them among the lodges would create sounds that might wake the sleeping camp. Instead she led the way across the shallow riffle of the stream. In the meadow beyond, the shadowy forms of horses grazed in the dim starlight.

They paused, trying to locate the sentry that they knew must be here somewhere. A man coughed and both pointed silently. He was leaning against a tree a few paces upstream.

"Give me time to get behind him," Long Walker whispered.

Running Eagle nodded and slipped the small knife into his palm. He stepped into the stream again to wade nearer their quarry.

The girl waited a few moments, then stepped boldly

into the open. Instantly the sentry was on the alert, weapon ready.

"*Aiee*," she spoke as she turned toward him, smiling in the almost darkness. "I am looking for Black Fox," she told him in sign talk when she was closer. "Have you seen him?"

The man chuckled. The entire camp was aware of the events of the day and that the beautiful prisoner had prepared herself to go to Black Fox's bed. The sentry relaxed, and she could almost feel his leer in the darkness.

"He is not here." Another suggestive chuckle. "If I were Black Fox, I would not be hard to find."

Taking the cue, she moved toward him suggestively. "Could you help me?"

By now the man was practically helpless. Walker's arm circled his throat to keep him from crying out, and the little knife flashed.

"*Aiee*, he is well armed," Walker commented.

He gathered the bow and arrows and handed them to the girl. "Here. You are better with these."

From its place against the tree, he took a short lance and hefted it for balance. The man had also carried a light war club, which now Long Walker hung at his own waist.

The two moved into the horse herd, searching for likely mounts. It was difficult in the darkness, but there was little time to choose. At any moment Little Bird might become curious about Running Eagle's long absence and give the alarm.

Each selected an animal and circled the jaw with a thong brought from Black Fox's lodge. Together they swung to the horses' backs.

It was important now to move quietly until well away from the herd. The horses must not become excited and noisy and wake the sleeping camp.

They followed the stream for a long bow-shot's distance, then entered the shallow water to hide their tracks as they traveled downstream. When they emerged

at a rocky crossing, they immediately entered a meadow
of tall grass to further confuse the trail.

Finally they were able to ascend to the flat table of
the upland, where they traveled rapidly. Not until
long afterward did they pause to rest their horses and
themselves. Exhausted from the stress and their
exertions, they stretched flat on the crest of a ridge
that would give them a view of the back trail.

"It is good to ride together again, Walker. Thank
you for coming."

"It was nothing," he answered.

Beyond that, he did not speak. Some things were
better unsaid.

At daybreak they studied the area they had crossed
and found no sign of enemy pursuit. It was as expected; the Head Splitters must wait until daylight to
search for the trail.

They remounted and moved on. They circled, back-
tracked, crossed a long slope of loose rock, waded
another stream—all to confuse the enemy pursuit. All
of their movements, however, took the same general
direction, back toward the camp of their own band.

During their stops to rest and let the horses graze,
they talked of many things, but not of the thing closest to the heart of Long Walker: What now? He was
afraid to broach the subject, and the girl did not do so.

Was her mission complete, he wondered, her vows
fulfilled? Surely she had wrought enough vengeance
for her brother's death. She had struck down enough
of the enemy for one lifetime. The last time the subject had come between them, though, was an unpleasant time. He would wait.

Before dark fell, Long Walker killed a fat yearling
buffalo bull, and they risked a fire to cook and eat.

They were ravenously hungry and consumed great
quantities of meat. Their fire was kept small, and they
carefully chose the driest of fuel to hold the smoke to
a minimum. Its blaze was allowed to subside before
full darkness to avoid the reflection of firelight in the
night.

The fugitives huddled together for warmth, but both were cautious. Neither wished to risk the misunderstanding that had resulted from close physical contact previously.

With the first light of dawn they were on the move again. It would be several sleeps before they reached the relative safety of their own tribe's area of influence.

They made no effort to conceal evidence of their stop. Scavengers had stripped the bull's carcass during the night, and already circling buzzards were dropping to investigate any remaining fragments.

Their fire's evidence could not be concealed. The ashes would remain until the next rain, but there seemed little likelihood that they were pursued anyway. In the more relaxed situation, they began to converse, to enjoy each other again, in a way that had not occurred for several moons. Long Walker was encouraged but did not attempt to press the advantage. Their talk was of trivial things, the beauty of the day, the spicy smell of the prairie in autumn, and the treasured memories of their childhood together.

Running Eagle still avoided all mention of her plans for the future. Actually she did so from reluctance to face the questions that the future held. For so long she had felt trapped in a series of events where she had had no choice, no control over her life. Now the thought that it was over, that she could make decisions in her life's direction, was a difficult one.

It was easier merely to ride with Long Walker to enjoy his companionship, to eat, to sleep, and to enjoy the warm sunlight of the quiet days. The girl did not realize that she was refusing to face the choices that she must make.

However, another discovery as they traveled suddenly eliminated the need to think of the future. They had stopped on the crest of a wind-swept ridge to rest and survey the distant prairie.

The distant blue haze of earth's rim was more than a day's travel away in all directions. There were the myriad sounds of the grassland and the scattered herds of buffalo, elk, and the occasional antelope. A yellow-breasted lark sang his chortling song from a nearby stone, and all seemed well.

Then suddenly Long Walker, who had been studying their back trail, stepped to the top of a boulder for better view.

"*Aiee*, Running Eagle! They come!"

She followed his pointing finger. There, less than a half-day's easy travel away, a line of mounted warriors filed over the ridge and moved rapidly toward them.

The girl's spirits fell in despair. Would this never end?

38
>> >> >>

No sooner had the fugitives spotted their pursuers than they wordlessly reached for the reins that dangled from their horses' mouths. They swung to the animals' backs and kicked their respective mounts into a speedy retreat.

It was a matter of great concern to discover that they were still followed, even at a great distance. The Head Splitters had apparently adjusted and organized much more rapidly than they had anticipated. Running Eagle attempted to retrace the events surrounding their escape.

Little Bird had undoubtedly lain in her bed and seethed with anger and jealousy. The woman would have been so resentful that she was happy, perhaps, for the absence of the prisoner from the lodge. It was even possible that she may have wished the captive to escape, so that she, Little Bird, could have her man back again. Even better, the prisoner might be killed in the escape attempt. Running Eagle could follow this sequence of events and see why the woman would be reluctant to thwart an escape.

It seemed unlikely that either of the wives of Black Fox had been aware of the small knife that she had hidden. *Aiee*, it had happened so rapidly. Long Walker had barely handed her the blade when Black Fox shouted, and she had been forced to rid herself of the object. She had tucked it beneath the edge of the buffalo skin she had been working. The skin remained pegged to the ground, and the knife had been there to recover when she needed it.

It was unlikely, in fact, that the death of Black Fox was even discovered until morning. Then a great cry must have occurred and the disappearance of the prisoners discovered. When horses were reported missing, one of the other subchiefs, perhaps a friend of Black Fox, would organize a pursuit.

At that point Running Eagle could not see how the enemy had followed them so rapidly. They had taken great pains to confuse the back trail for any possible trackers.

There was only one possible explanation. After the first day of fruitless search and aimless attempts to sort out the conflicting signs, the enemy had deciphered their strategy. Someone, perhaps the leader of the pursuit party, was intelligent enough to look beyond the immediate. He had reasoned that they must rejoin their people. Therefore the pursuers had abandoned the effort to unravel the deliberately false signs of retreat. They had pushed rapidly forward in the only direction possible, toward the fugitives' own country.

Now the pursuit party had nearly overtaken them, and Running Eagle realized that the situation was desperate. The enemy had probably not seen them yet but were undoubtedly following their trail. For the past two suns they had made no effort to conceal their tracks.

Their main concern had been the welfare of their horses. The animals would normally spend more than half the day in grazing. While they traveled, it was impossible for the horses to do so. There was simply insufficient time during the brief stops for sleep and rest.

Already the animals were beginning to appear gaunt. It had been intended to allow them to rest and fatten again when they reached safety.

But that was several sleeps away, and Running Eagle and Long Walker had struck a moderate compromise. They had slowed their flight enough to keep the horses in fair condition and still move steadily away from any possible pursuit. All had seemed well, until now. But their mounts were far from the quality needed for this sort of a chase. They had been forced to take animals they could catch, certainly not the best of the herd. The aging gelding ridden by Long Walker was only a shade poorer in stamina than the wind-broken mare which Running Eagle had obtained in the dark.

As long as their flight had been one of subterfuge instead of speed, the animals had been adequate. Barely adequate, of course.

Now escape would depend on speed and stamina. Their pursuers would be well mounted, carrying adequate supplies. Running Eagle and Long Walker would be riding broken-down horses, already suffering from lack of grazing time. They had no supplies and could not stop to hunt.

Their chances of survival seemed to be diminishing rapidly. It was only a matter of time now until the enemy pursuit overtook them.

There would be no bargaining this time. Black Fox, with his strange, twisted preoccupation over the capture of Running Eagle, was dead. Their present pursuers would be looking for vengeance. Vengeance and the need to eliminate the threat of the warrior woman, once and for all, from the prairie.

Running Eagle was exhausted. It was not so much a physical tiredness as the fact that her very spirit cried out for rest. For as long as she could remember, it seemed, an urgency had been hanging over her. She had had no opportunity to rest, to renew her spirit.

Always some urgent thing had pressed her to action in which she had no real decisions.

Her vision quest should have provided this pause, she now realized. In some way, as she looked back, she felt that she had misused her vision quest. Her mind had been busy with her plans and goals instead of allowing her spirit guide to find her. She wished that she could try again.

The tired horses clattered over a ridge, and Running Eagle turned to look backward. There, somewhat closer now, came the enemy column. The determined, fast pace indicated that the fugitives had been seen. It was as if the enemy party, bent on vengeance, recognized that this was the last push. Before Sun Boy's torch dropped below earth's rim, the end would come.

Her morose thoughts were interrupted by an exclamation from Long Walker. *"Aiee! Look!"*

He pointed ahead, pulling his horse to a stop. There, crossing the floor of the valley, came another column of riders. They were well-armed, efficient-looking warriors, mounted on strong horses.

Running Eagle pulled her horse to the right and sprinted along the crest of the ridge, followed closely by Long Walker. In a short while they were forced to a stop again. A broken gash across the ridge dropped sharply away to jumbled rocks below.

Again they turned the sweating horses, reversing direction to seek escape. To the right and left the approaching war parties could be seen. Running Eagle held no delusions as to their real possibilities for success. The ridge ended in a long, fingerlike projection above a level strip of grass along the stream. The fugitives would make their way down from the point, but then they would still be between the two groups of warriors and pinned against the stream. Perhaps they could cross.

Another look at the lathered horses told her that this was, at best, an unlikely possibility. Her own mount, in all probability, could not even reach the stream.

Both groups had seen the riders on the ridge now and were veering in that direction. Already the yipping falsetto war cry of the Head Splitters could be heard in the distance.

It could be seen that the newly discovered column of warriors would reach the apex of the ridge's point well in advance of the pursuit group. The fugitives would have to confront them first. Running Eagle turned to look as she rode, evaluating their slim chances against such a well-equipped and efficient war party as this appeared to be.

The leading riders were almost even with them now, though far below in the flat meadow. Their leader appeared to be making signals of some sort with broad waves of his arm.

"Running Eagle!" Long Walker shouted suddenly. "Look! They are the People!"

She pulled her panting horse to a stop to better her view of the riders. It was true. The well-armed war party wore the garments and distinctive hair style of warriors of their own tribe. The young chief in the lead was none other than Flying Squirrel.

39
» »» »

Running Eagle returned the warrior's wave and turned her horse down the slope.

"*Ah-koh*, Running Eagle! It is good to see you!" The smile on the face of Flying Squirrel was broad and happy.

"Flying Squirrel!" she cried urgently. "The Head Splitters are just behind us!"

More riders were approaching, pulling to a stop, shouting and singing, "We ride with Running Eagle!"

How quickly things change, the girl thought briefly. But now, they must prepare quickly.

"My friends!" she shouted. "There are Head Splitters on the other side of the ridge. We must hurry!"

There was a chorus of shouts, but she held up a hand for silence. In the pause that followed, the distant yipping cry of the Head Splitters came floating across the prairie.

Then an idea struck her. The Head Splitters, on the other side of the ridge, were not yet aware of Flying

Squirrel's party. In a short while they would burst around the point of the hill, believing that they were in hot pursuit of two fugitives on exhausted horses. Even at the time the humor of the situation struck her. But they must hurry. Rapidly she outlined the situation.

Running Eagle and Long Walker once again called on weakening horses to lope toward the stream, a few hundred paces away. They rode slowly, attempting to save the animals for a last burst of strength. As they neared the thin strip of trees along the bank, a victorious shout came from beyond the hill. Now the two were in full view of the approaching enemy party.

They paused and, as if in confused terror, turned to retrace their course, striving to return to the slight protection of the hill. The leading riders were gaining rapidly and pressed ahead, wishing to achieve the prestige of counting first honors against the fabled pair.

It is likely that, as the Head Splitters rounded the point of land, the last thing the leaders saw was a closely massed party of mounted warriors, poised for attack. A shower of arrows emptied saddles, and yipping war cries changed to screams of the wounded.

The next rank of attacking Head Splitters paused in confusion. Some turned back, others stopped, and a few pushed forward. Riderless horses milled around in confusion.

Into this melee thundered the main thrust of the People's charge. Young warriors lowered lance points or fitted arrows to bowstrings and urged their horses forward.

In the center of the attacking line rode Running Eagle and Long Walker. The war cry of the People swelled across the meadow.

In the face of this organized and completely unexpected attack, the Head Splitters turned and ran. Their leaders were already unhorsed, dead or dying, and complete confusion reigned. The greatest desire of many inexperienced young warriors was now to escape. A few tried to stand and fight, but they were quickly overrun.

The People rode up and down the little valley, making certain that no remaining enemy were able to pose a danger.

Running Eagle had stopped after the first clash, out of concern for her staggering horse. She dismounted, using her bow with great effectiveness when opportunity offered. Long Walker stood at her side, ready to protect her against any threat.

Dust hung in the air, and its taste was dry and bitter. As the excitement and urgency of the situation began to calm somewhat, Running Eagle's exhaustion became overwhelming. She resisted the impulse to run from the scene. She had not slept for two days, during which there had been constant physical and emotional exertion.

True, there had been a moment of exhilaration when she and Long Walker were able to decoy the Head Splitters into the trap, but it was gone. There was no joy in the victory.

She looked across the meadow, at the still forms in the grass. There was none of the triumph she had once felt. Even the satisfaction of revenge was absent. There was only the smell of death.

She looked down at the weapon in her hand. It seemed foreign to her nature. In that moment she realized that it was over. She was finished with vengeance, with the trail of war. If she fought again, it would be only for defense.

Warriors began to return, singing and yelling, carrying captured weapons and leading riderless horses. This would be a great victory to be remembered in song and dance for many generations.

And in their songs of victory the main theme recurred, that of the invincible warrior woman who escaped the enemy and led them into a trap. Always the triumphant chorus ended with the same phrase: "We ride with Running Eagle!"

With a sinking heart, the girl felt again the desperate, trapped emotion, the feeling that she had no choice in the matter. She squared her shoulders and raised her hand with the bow and arrows in acknowledgment of their song.

40
>> >> >>

It was nearing evening now. The People had moved a short distance upstream to make camp and allow the Head Splitters to recover their dead. The defeated enemy party could still be seen in the distance, lifting and carrying away their fallen.

The casualties among the People had been light—a few minor wounds, and one man killed in the first charge. The enemy had been far too concerned with running after that.

Camp fires were blossoming in the gathering dusk. Running Eagle beckoned to her companion. "Come, Walker. Let us talk."

The two strolled together along the stream. Long Walker was very quiet. The silence was clumsy, but neither could find a way to approach the subject that weighed heavily on both their minds. Both knew this was a time of decision. Long Walker had raised the question many times and now would not do so again.

In truth he was afraid to do so, afraid that he had already lost her. He had seen the thrill of excitement in her eyes when the enemy followed them into the trap. There was little doubt that she was impressed by the songs of devotion by her followers. No one could fail to be flattered.

Walker felt much of the same hopelessness that the girl had experienced. He, too, had had little choice for many moons. Now he was wondering. Could he look forward to little more than a lifetime of following Running Eagle, protecting her as best he might? He could not see himself settling down in his own lodge with any other woman. Yet Running Eagle seemed always more unattainable.

The girl, in turn, was equally troubled. She knew that she had repeatedly caused Long Walker to be hurt deeply. She had no wish to hurt him more. There was also the very real danger that the decision she had made in the twilight of the prairie evening would drive him forever away from her. She hesitated to risk this possibility, so she, too, remained silent.

They walked along the stream, listening to its soft, rippling conversation with the overhanging willows. The creek tumbled across a white gravel bar and sank softly into a still pool ringed by rushes on the opposite bank. A great frog tentatively voiced his booming call from somewhere in the deepening dusk.

The sky in the west was still red, but the noises of the prairie were changing. Bird and insect songs of the daylight hours were giving way to the sounds of the night. A fish splashed in the still darkness beneath an overhanging willow. Further away a night bird began his mournful chorus. A coyote called his chuckling wail from a distant ridge, and his mate answered from another quarter.

Near the gravel bar a fallen sycamore lay, and the two sat on its trunk to rest. Running Eagle absently picked up a stone from beneath her feet, toying with it in her hands.

"Walker," she began, "we must talk."

He nodded, miserably.

The girl hesitated, not knowing where to begin.

One could not just blurt out such things, things on which their entire future depended.

She held the stone in her palm. It was comforting to hold, smooth, round, and still warm from the sun. It fit nicely in her hand. Gently she held it against her cheek, feeling its smooth surface and comforting warmth.

"What is that?" Walker inquired.

Meaningless conversation was better than the awkward silence.

"Only a stone. I thought I might keep it."

She smiled at him in the almost darkness, still rubbing the stone against the skin of her cheek. "It will make a good cooking stone."

For only a moment Long Walker was silent, trying to be certain of her meaning. Then he gently took the stone from her hand, held it, and hefted it. He smiled.

"Yes," he agreed. "Shall I help you find more?"

ABOUT THE AUTHOR

DON COLDSMITH was born in Iola, Kansas, in 1926. He served as a World War II combat medic in the South Pacific and returned to his native state where he graduated from Baker University in 1949 and received his M.D. from the University of Kansas in 1958. He worked at several jobs before entering medical school: he was a YMCA group counselor, a gunsmith, a taxidermist, and for a short time, a Congregational preacher. In addition to his private medical practice, Dr. Coldsmith is a staff physician at Emporia State University's Health Center, teaches in the English Department, and is active as a freelance writer, lecturer, and rancher. He and his wife of 26 years, Edna, have raised five daughters.

Dr. Coldsmith produced the first ten novels in "The Spanish Bit Saga" in a five-year period; he writes and revises the stories first in his head, then in longhand. From this manuscript he reads aloud to his wife, whom he calls his "chief editor." Finally the finished version is skillfully typed by his longtime office receptionist.

Of his decision to create, or re-create, the world of the Plains Indian in the 16th and 17th centuries, the author says: "There has been very little written about this time period. I wanted also to portray these Native Americans as human beings, rather than as stereotyped 'Indians.' That word does not appear anywhere in the series—for a reason. As I have researched the time and place of the indigenous cultures, it's been a truly inspiring experience for me."

A Proud People In a Beautiful Land

THE SPANISH BIT SAGA

Set on the Great Plains of North America in the 16th through 18th centuries, Don Coldsmith's acclaimed series recreates a time, a place and a people that have been nearly lost to history. Here is history in the making through the eyes of the proud Native Americans who lived it.